The Little Yokozuna

By Wayne Shorey

TUTTLE PUBLISHING
Boston · Rutland, Vermont · Tokyo

First published in 2003 by Tuttle Publishing, an imprint of Periplus Editions (HK) Ltd., with editorial offices at 153 Milk Street, Boston, Massachusetts 02109.

Library of Congress Cataloging-in-Publication Data

LCC Card Number: 2002075061
Shorey, Wayne.
The little Yokozuna / Wayne Shorey
1st ed.
Boston, Mass. : Tuttle Pub., 2003.
p. cm.

ISBN: 0-8048-3479-2

Distributed by:

North America, Latin America, and Europe
Tuttle Publishing Distribution Center
Airport Industrial Park
364 Innovation Drive
North Clarendon, VT 05759-9436
Tel: (802) 773-8930
Fax: (802) 773-6993
Email:info@tuttlepublishing.com

Japan
Tuttle Publishing
Yaekari Bldg., 3F
5-4-12 Ōsaki, Shinagawa-ku
Tokyo 141-0032
Tel: (03) 5437-0171
Fax: (03) 5437-0755
Email: tuttle-sales@gol.com

Asia Pacific
Berkeley Books Pte. Ltd.
130 Joo Seng Road
#06-01/03 Olivine Building
Singapore 368357
Tel: (65) 6280-3220
Fax: (65) 6280-6290
Email: inquiries@periplus.com.sg

First edition
08 07 06 05 04 03   9 8 7 6 5 4 3 2 1

Design by Serena Fox Design
Printed in Canada

CONTENTS

CHAPTER 1

Something Happens to Kiyoshi-chan

There was once a young boy named Kiyoshi-chan, who was born in a village called Kashiwa, in the ancient country of Japan, and who then had nothing happen to him for the first eleven years of his life.

If this sort of thing had gone on, of course, there would be no story to tell about Kiyoshi-chan, since for a story to *be* a story something has to *happen*. But as it came about, there finally was a certain rainy night when everything seemed to start happening to Kiyoshi-chan at once, changing his life forever.

At the time of this adventure, Kiyoshi-chan would have said that he was eleven years old. The reason for this is that from olden times, when the Japanese count age they include the year of life inside the mother's womb, before the child is born. Kiyoshi-chan liked this custom. American children would have called him ten, which would have hurt Kiyoshi-chan's pride a bit, but there it is.

By the time he was eleven, then, Kiyoshi-chan had learned to love several things above all else. First, he loved the great sport of sumo with a grand passion. Six times a year he watched the Grand Sumo Tournaments on the little black-and-white TV his father kept in the quilt closet, and he could never stop talking about his favorite *rikishi*, or sumo wrestlers. He had actually attended several of the great tournaments in person, awed by the pageantry and by the presence of some of history's most famous wrestlers. "I am one of the luckiest Japanese boys *ever*," he said one day, when he was much younger. "Why is that?" his mother asked. "Because I live in the days of Taiho, the greatest *yokozuna* of all time," he said. "Think of all the boys in olden times who never heard of Taiho, or the boys in the future who will wish they had seen him. I am in *just* the right time of history."

And how many people can say that, believing it?

Next to sumo, Kiyoshi-chan loved baseball, and in a very different way he loved his family. But sumo was his grand passion.

Speaking of Kiyoshi-chan's family, there were six people in it, living in a small warm space no bigger than sixteen *tatami* mats. There were his father, his mother, Kiyoshi-chan himself, and his little sister Izumi-chan. But there were also his *obaa-san* and *ojii-san*, his grandmother and grandfather, who had lived forever in their own tiny two-mat room, bent in half and full of wrinkles.

Kiyoshi-chan never noticed the inside of his home, just because he had always lived there. It would have been harder to describe for him than his mother's face, just because he knew it so well. Someone else would have noticed the four tiny rooms, the dark beams and white plaster, the sliding paper doors, the *genkan* or entryway for shoes, the *tatami,* which was just right for sitting on, neither too hard nor too soft. Someone else would have smelled the particular smell of the place, which by now belonged to Kiyoshi-chan as much as his nose did, the smell of *tatami* and rice and fish and *miso*, all blended together in a way that would have seemed perfect to Kiyoshi-chan, if he had ever thought about it.

As with all Japanese homes, Kiyoshi-chan's began at the gate to its tiny yard. Inside and outside were equally part of the home, with only a low threshold and sliding doors to separate them. The outside part of Kiyoshi-chan's home was only the size of eight *tatami* mats, and was mostly covered with mouse-colored dirt that his mother swept free of footprints every day. It was enclosed by a high bamboo fence and thick shrubs that reached almost as high as the red roof tiles, which made their home as private and secret as a woodchuck's.

Since Kiyoshi-chan's yard was no bigger than a medium-sized room, it might seem to have been too small to have a garden. But in the corner of the yard was an arrangement of rocks and tiny trees that his father had set up, with great reverence. He had explained carefully to Kiyoshi-chan how he was trying to show the whole universe in this one little garden, and how each stone was a mountain, and the tiny stream of white pebbles a rushing river, and a waterfall. He had explained the difference between a crane-shaped stone and a turtle-shaped stone, and how the arrangement of stones told a special story from long ago.

Kiyoshi-chan heard this well, and tried to understand it, especially trying to take it as seriously as his father said it. How could the whole Universe fit into one little garden? Even his *school* was too big to hold in his mind all at once. And he knew that the Universe also included Wakamatsu-san's market, the train station, the vacant lot where he played baseball, and all of Kashiwa, Tokyo, Japan, and the whole world besides. Kiyoshi-chan's face wore a philosophical squint as he wrestled with this, making his father laugh. Kiyoshi-chan laughed, too, but there were actually moments when he felt a little sorry for his father for suggesting the whole idea. It was the first time he had ever caught his parents in anything like a mistake, and it made him melancholy for a day.

One Monday, after school, Kiyoshi-chan walked home the usual way, through a steady March rain. The school was two streets away, one of them loud and blaring with bicycles and little three-wheeled trucks. The next street was quieter, running between two cement-block walls, and Kiyoshi-chan kicked his way along through the puddles and the dusk, comfortable in his yellow raincoat and bright blue boots. He passed a tiny restaurant that was just a bright door in the wall, and saw through it two men sitting at the only table, eating noodles with chopsticks and talking loudly. The warmth and smell of food spilled out onto Kiyoshi-chan, making him think of his mother and supper, so he began to run, up the street, over the roadside gutter, through the gate, along the narrow covered pathway between the houses, and into his yard.

There in his yard were the light of home and the smell of food again, and rain falling all around. Something made him stop and stand still as a stone, hearing and smelling the rain with his whole self, the water streaming off his hat brim and around his face like a veil. He lifted his hands out to either side and let the rain beat on the yellow sleeves of his raincoat.

Then suddenly he noticed his father's garden.

It was different.

Kiyoshi-chan looked at it, perplexed. What was different about it?

He went over and squatted down on his heels, with his bottom only an inch from the streaming stepping-stones. He looked hard at the garden. There were the usual shrubs and trees, the river and pool of pebbles carefully raked into ripples, moss growing in little mounds and over the stone lantern. Everything was there, in its place. The stones were dark with rain, and three ancient little trees dripped into the moss.

Kiyoshi-chan shuffled forward on his boots, inch by inch, and peered behind the lantern into the shadows of the tiny garden. In the dusk and rain, the shadows under the old dwarf pine trees seemed deeper than usual, as if they were hiding mysteries. Kiyoshi-chan thought he felt a small piney breeze blowing out from under them, down the pebbly waterfall, through the rocks of the miniature ravine, into his face. He felt a pang of gladness again, as he had when he had first come into the yard. For a moment he could almost imagine tiny deer moving among the trees, hawks the size of gnats soaring around the mountaintops. He leaned forward until his nose was almost touching the dripping pine needles, and closed his eyes, using his nose to hunt for another breath of piney mountain wind.

He had no idea how long he stayed there. His soul seemed to go out from him through his nose and wander through the wilderness of the garden, a tiny pilgrim with a staff and a great straw rain hat. The dusk had almost turned to complete darkness when his worried mother finally came out and discovered him.

"Kiyoshi-chan," she said, touching him on the shoulder. He jumped to his feet and shouted. His mother held him tightly, now truly alarmed. "Are you all right, Kiyoshi-chan? What is wrong?"

He was embarrassed. "Nothing, mama," he said, burying his face in her old familiar house kimono. "You startled me, that's all."

As he followed her inside, she laughed for only themselves to hear, to make him feel better. "When I first saw you there," she said, "I thought your father had added a new stone to the garden. A second crane-stone to keep the Old One company."

At the door, Kiyoshi-chan looked back one last time at his father's garden, and stopped with one foot already over the threshold and one still outside. He peered out into the dark. Did something move there behind the lantern, under the little pines? Did he see a quick glimmer of eyes? He thought of foxes, and bears, and demons, and was filled with fear. Stepping in quickly, he slid the door shut behind him.

CHAPTER 2

Night Sounds

Late that night, Kiyoshi-chan lay on his futon, wide-awake. Izumi-chan was asleep beside him, her face looking very white in the night, almost as if it were shining like a small moon. The rain was still running back and forth over the roof tiles, like ghostly children playing kickball, but it was not the rain that was keeping Kiyoshi-chan awake.

Kiyoshi-chan was remembering part of what had made him feel so happy earlier, when he had first returned home. He had been even gladder than usual ever since yesterday after school, when he had finally beaten the big twelve-year-old Taro-chan in the after-school sumo wrestling at the playground. Taro-chan was so big and strong that he usually beat Kiyoshi-chan with a ridiculous move, lifting the smaller boy up by the seat of his pants and setting him outside the ring like a baby. Then he would dust off his hands like a real sumo wrestler.

"For your information," Taro-chan would always say, "that was a lovely *tsuridashi*." He was proud to know the names of all the sumo techniques, from *uwatenage* to *yorikiri*. But a *tsuridashi* was to lift up an opponent by his belt, or *mawashi*, and to set him outside the ring. Everyone would laugh at Taro-chan's treatment of Kiyoshi-chan, knowing that they would soon have their turns to lose. Taro-chan was always the champion of the playground.

But yesterday Kiyoshi-chan had gone after Taro-chan like a fury, hooked his leg and pushed him over backward with all his might before the large boy had a chance to grab him. "Oof!" Taro-chan had grunted as he landed on his bottom, like a fat sack of rice. He sat there with a look of pure amazement on his face, his eyes as round as rice bowls.

Then Kiyoshi-chan had turned to the circle of astonished boys and carefully dusted his hands. "For your information," he said. "That was a lovely *kawazugake*."

Then everyone crowed at Kiyoshi-chan's great victory. Even Taro-chan got to his feet with a crooked smile and bowed with great dignity to Kiyoshi-chan, and Kiyoshi-chan grinned till his cheeks hurt.

Now tonight Kiyoshi-chan could not sleep for thinking about his victory over Taro-chan, and he laughed out loud again.

"Why are you laughing, Kiyoshi-chan?" asked his father from the other side of the paper doors. "Are you dreaming or awake?"

"I'm awake, papa," said Kiyoshi-chan. "I'm remembering Taro-chan yesterday."

He heard both his mother and father laugh in the other room.

"Go to sleep, Taiho," said his father.

"Skinny little *yokozuna*," said his mother.

So Kiyoshi-chan tried to go to sleep, but his mind was too wide awake to let his body drift away. He remembered how when the boys had finished praising him for his victory, the talk had turned to American baseball and the new season. They had talked about Bob Gibson, the great pitcher of the world champion St. Louis Cardinals, and about the amazing left fielder of the Boston Red Sox, whose name was too long and hard to pronounce. They just called him *Yazu*. Kiyoshi-chan loved baseball, but not as much as he loved sumo, and he wished they would talk of Taiho and Kashiwado and Sadanoyama instead, or even the wrestler Wakachichibu, who was as big as a mountain and who wobbled as he walked.

The night hours passed, the rain fell, and Kiyoshi-chan thought of many things while the whole house slept around him. Finally, in all the circling of his memories, he remembered the strange experience in his father's garden last evening. He tried to puzzle out what had been different about the garden, or if it were just the extra reflections of the rain that had made it seem depthless, as if his father's garden really was full of the Universe.

Then he heard the child crying.

At first he thought it was Izumi-chan making sounds in her sleep, so he turned to see what was wrong. But her face was still as round and white and silent as the moon, and she had a look as if she were dreaming pleasant dreams.

Then he thought it was a cat, and tried to close his eyes again to go to sleep. Their neighbors had a cat who sometimes came into their yard under the bamboo fence. It must be a very wet cat tonight, thought Kiyoshi-chan.

But then his eyes sprang open again. It didn't really sound at all like a cat when he listened closely. As he lay there and heard the strange sound go on, something brought back to him the thought of last night's garden and of its shadows, strangely fathomless and frightening. It was no child crying, he thought suddenly. It was a ghost or a demon, trying to lure him outside. He burrowed under his quilt, his heart thumping in his ears.

But still it went on and on, like the saddest whimpering of a hurt beast, just loud enough now and then for him to hear it between the waves of rain. Kiyoshi-chan felt the sadness of it deep down in his stomach, and wanted to cry with it as if it were the voice of some universal sorrow. Silly person, he had to remind himself. He had no sorrow at all to speak of, and he had beaten Taro-chan with a lovely *kawazugake* yesterday. Why should he feel like crying?

Feeling brave, Kiyoshi-chan pushed back his quilt and stood up. He would go and see what the sound was, and he wouldn't wake his parents. He slid back the door of their room and padded in his bare feet around their futon. In the entryway he slipped on his father's great wooden *geta*, so his feet would stay out of the wet. Then he slid back the screen door and the wooden outer door, and stepped onto the outside platform. The rain poured off the roof like a curtain in front of his eyes. It was dark in the yard, but not as dark as he would have expected deep night to be.

He stepped forward to the edge of the platform and looked to the right, toward the gate and away from his father's garden. Somehow it seemed to him that if there was anything to see it would be in the garden, but he almost stepped back into the house without looking in that direction, as if he had done all he could do. He stopped himself with an exasperated exclamation, but still found himself reluctant to look where he knew he needed to.

"Remember Taro-chan!" he said aloud. He grinned at himself for doing it, but knew that in a world where such things happened, he could not step back now. With determination, he went right to the edge of the platform and peered through the dreary darkness into the shadows where his father's garden was. For a moment he could see nothing.

Then he screamed at the top of his lungs. Something moved in the deep shadows, and then out from under the tiny trees of the garden came a small white figure, a ghost surely. He screamed again.

The ghost seemed paralyzed by his scream, and they stared frozen at each other, the boy and his ghost. Part of Kiyoshi-chan's mind noticed that it wasn't really a ghost, it was a very, very wet little girl of about four years old, with yellow hair and white, white skin, with even greater terror than his on her face. Kiyoshi-chan barely had a chance to begin to stop screaming when the little girl did the strangest thing he could ever have expected. She suddenly held her nose and sprang into the air, cannonballing to the ground. But instead of thumping with a splat onto her bottom in the mud, she disappeared into the earth as if it were water. A couple of thick ripples spread out and dissipated along the surface of the ground.

Kiyoshi-chan was too shocked to scream any more. He stared at the place where the little girl had been, but now the yard was dark and empty, streaming with rain and ghostless. He stood like a statue on the edge of the platform, with the rain pouring down onto the front of his head.

"Kiyoshi-chan!" said his father behind him. "What in the *world* are you doing out here?"

CHAPTER 3

Knuckleball
Takes a Swing

By the time Kiyoshi-chan finished telling his parents about the little girl-ghost in the garden, he could hardly keep his eyes open. His mother led him back to his futon, covered him with his warm quilt, and smiled to see him already sound asleep. But even as the little home grew quiet under the hypnotic rain, something else was already happening, and not far away. Two strange children were walking in the nighttime down-pour along Kiyoshi-chan's own Kashiwa street, with no idea in the world where they were.

"I don't know how we're ever gonna find her, Granny," said a boy named Knuckleball, who was the same age as Kiyoshi-chan, but didn't know it, of course. He also had the name of Edward, but was called Knuckleball because of always trying to throw one when he played catch with anybody. He was wearing crooked wire-rimmed glasses, and a shapeless, battered baseball cap that made his hair stick out over his ears in wild ways. It had been a long time since he'd had a haircut. "I mean, let's face it," he went on, trudging through a big puddle just for fun, "we have no clue where we've landed this time. Just look at this rain, Gran. Where does it rain a lot? How about Seattle? Do you think this is Seattle? But Seattle's in America, isn't it? And this doesn't look like any part of America I've ever seen, no way. Just when we think we know where we are we get blown a million miles off course. Doesn't that just figure, Gran?"

His companion said nothing. She was a tall, slender teenager who walked with a dancer's graceful stride, and she looked like she had been out in the rain for days. Her face, normally puckish and pleasant, was now set and somber. She had tied her blond hair back with an old shoelace, and her jeans were torn at the knees. Her name was Annie, and she was Knuckleball's sister.

"Scratch Seattle," said Knuckleball. "Let's see, what other cities do I know about? It's obviously not Boston, or Philadelphia, or London. We've been to those places, and they're nothing like this. A little more traffic, I think, even this time of night. What about Chicago? Does it rain in Chicago? I mean, I was barely born when we lived in Chicago, and was hardly checking the weather, Gran, but you must have noticed, huh?"

"Whatever," said Annie.

They stopped at a junction of narrow ways. There were no streetlights and all the houses were dark. The rain poured from the black sky and gushed along the street gutters.

"Knuckles," said Annie. "We already know where we are."

"You mean we had a *theory* where we *were*," said Knuckleball. "I think this last little trip of ours cooked that theory pretty good, not that it was *ever* that definite to begin with. Now we've been blown into the

Twilight Zone. You watch, any minute we'll find ourselves walking sideways into our own ears or something. Wouldn't that be cool?"

Annie said nothing but kept walking, peering into the gloom. Her shoes squelched.

"So," said Knuckleball, "until we find out for sure that we've fallen into a parallel universe, we'll assume that this is Earth and just start trying to figure out what continent we're on. You go ahead and enjoy the rain, Granny. I'll handle the brainwork."

"Mm," said Annie.

"Thank you for your support," said Knuckleball, straightening his crooked glasses for the hundredth time.

"And my name is not Granny," said Annie.

"Okeydoke," said Knuckleball, shoving his hands into his pockets and stomping in another puddle. "Annie Granny, quite uncanny," he chanted in time to his marching.

"Knucklehead," said Annie, "do you ever, ever, ever stop talking?"

"Of *course* not," said the boy, appalled. "How could I do that to *everyone else*? They *depend* on me, Gran."

"Well," said Annie.

"Besides, we can just stop this silly game anyway," said Knuckleball, kicking a pebble into the gutter, where it splashed with a hollow *thop*. "I know *exactly* where we are."

Annie pushed back her soaked bangs and blew at the runnel of rain pouring off the tip of her nose.

"I can't wait to hear this," she said. "Where . . ."

Then, to Knuckleball's intense astonishment, she suddenly stopped in the middle of her sentence, threw her hands in the air, and sat down in the middle of the road, as if it weren't raining in sheets all around her. Her brother gaped.

"Well, that doesn't look very comfortable," he said. "Can't we find a dry place to rest?"

Annie buried her face in her arms. It took a moment for Knuckleball to realize that she was crying. He knelt down beside her and hugged her awkwardly.

"Annie!" he said. "I'm really sorry! I'll stop talking so much."

"Knuckles," sobbed Annie. "Why would I care what you say?" Then she put her head down and cried some more, silently. Knuckleball flopped down in the road and leaned his back up against hers.

"We've been looking for her for so *long*," said Annie finally. "It's been so long since we saw her. I want to find her, and go home."

"I know," said Knuckleball. "I know."

The two children sat, back to back, on the street. The sound of the drumming rain seemed to fill their heads with an ever-louder roar until it numbed them and seemed more like a great hollow silence than a noise, the hushing of the vast Universe, a long syllable of emptiness, like the voice of the Ocean. Annie cried no more, but they sat on in the rain longer than either of them could tell.

It was out of the depths of this deep-voiced stillness that they heard it.

"I hear thunder," said Knuckleball.

"Maybe," said Annie.

The thunder, if it was thunder, went on and on without interruption, growing in volume. There was no lightning to punctuate it. It seemed to be coming from the way they had come, far away over the horizon.

"It doesn't sound like thunder," said Knuckleball. "Not really."

"Thunder doesn't just keep *on*," said Annie.

"I don't like it," said the boy.

The sound grew and grew, until Knuckleball had to put his hands over his ears.

"Annie!" he cried. "Where can we go?"

"If I don't know what it is," said Annie, "how can I know where to hide from it?"

Incredibly, the town around them seemed still to be sleeping. No lights were lit, no gates open for sleepy-eyed people to peek through in curiosity. The rumble grew until the pavement seemed to shake with it.

"Annie!" cried Knuckleball. "We have to run! We can't just stay here!"

He leaped to his feet and ran to the nearest gate, throwing it open. There, with his hand just reached out to unlatch the gate from the inside, was a boy of his own age, with black hair and cream-colored skin.

Knuckleball stared at the boy for three heartbeats.

"Annie!" he yelled.

"What, Knuckler?" shouted Annie over the rain and the thunder, still rooted in the middle of the road and staring into the far distance.

"I know where we are!" cried Knuckleball.

"So do I!" said Annie.

From just inside the gate, Kiyoshi-chan stared out at the scene in the road. For a second time that night he had run out of his sleeping home, this time for the strange thunder. He was not sure why he again had not awakened his parents, but had run straight out to the street to see what was happening. He knew earthquakes and thunder and could tell that this was neither. With the strange experience of the garden and the ghost fresh in his mind, he was irresistibly drawn to this new mystery.

But as strange as the uncanny thunder were the two creatures he saw in the road, shaggy and soaked and yellow-haired, a boy and a girl shouting at each other in gibberish. Kiyoshi-chan gawked at them. What else could happen in this night of bizarre things?

"Knuckleball!" cried Annie, with a new note in her voice, of terror or triumph or something else. "It's *him!*"

The something extra in her voice made Kiyoshi-chan look toward the north also, though he understood none of the sounds she made. What he saw made him almost faint away with fear.

Far, far up the walled street, at the point where the walls met in the distance, there was a leaping lighted thing approaching, bounding toward them at an incredible speed. The roar of thunder seemed to come from the crashing of its feet on the pavement, though it sounded more like a thousand elephants in full stampede. Nearer and nearer it came, till they could see its great head, hideous with gaping mouth, rampant hair, and an eerie light flickering all around. It ran on two legs like a human, and waved a long, curved, cruel sword in its fist.

"*Oni,*" whispered Kiyoshi-chan, in fascinated dread. "*Oni!*"

On came the warrior goblin, on, near and nearer. The roar of its coming rose all around like a tsunami.

"Annie! Run!" wailed Knuckleball. "*Hide!*"

But Annie stood in the middle of the way, like a slim young tree. She raised a fist in the face of the leaping monster.

"Where is she?" she cried. "What have you done with our sister?"

Then Knuckleball also overcame his fear and stepped out of the shadow of the gateway. "Yeah, where *is* Little Harriet?" he yelled at the top of his lungs. "*Who do you think you are?*"

The goblin rumbled with anger and waved its sword, so that a blast of flame blew Annie back against the concrete block wall. She flopped into the rushing gutter, where she struggled back up to her hands and knees. The demon whirled aside toward her and bent its horrible head as if to devour her.

Then Knuckleball was filled with the greatest wrath of his life. As if there was no other hope left in the world, he snatched up a fence post lying on the ground and ran into the road. Even as he swung back the club, the thought flickered through his mind that it was about the same weight and feel of his favorite baseball bat. Kiyoshi-chan gaped in horror at this little boy that would challenge an *oni* with a fence post.

"Have you lost our Little Harriet?" Knuckleball screamed at the goblin. "Who do you think you are, you big *pimple!*"

The strange flaming creature lifted its head to stare at Knuckleball, and bent down again toward the stunned Annie. Then with a furious cry, Knuckleball swung his club as if everything in the world depended on it. There was a great crack as he connected on that hideous forehead. The goblin's ghastly head leaped off its body and rolled away.

Stupefied, they all watched it roll down the pavement, trundling back and forth like a lopsided ball.

The towering demon stood up and grabbed at the space over its shoulders with both hands. Not finding its head, it gave a gobbling howl, then turned and fled back where it had come, leaping down the street until it vanished in the distance. Annie looked up at Knuckleball. Knuckleball looked back at Annie. The head of the goblin wobbled down the curve of the pavement and plopped into the gutter.

"Oh, my," said Knuckleball, looking at the post in his hands as if it were a piece of dynamite. "How did I do that?"

"Nice hit, little brother," said Annie, quietly. "But I'd also like to know how it could roar like that even without its head."

"And what *I* want to know," said Knuckleball, "is what he's done with our Little Harriet."

Annie looked where the demon had fled, toward the far horizon of tiled Kashiwa roofs. "Are we sure he's the same one?" she asked, half to herself. "Could there *be* more than one?"

"Look, Annie," said her brother. "We have company." They looked down the street.

Kiyoshi-chan had hauled the goblin's head out of the gutter and was looking inside it. Suddenly he started to laugh, and put the revolting thing over his own head. Knuckleball and Annie looked at him, disgusted and amazed. But then Kiyoshi-chan said something, his voice echoing and muffled.

"Annie!" said Knuckleball, pulling her to her feet. "He's speaking Japanese! We *are* in Japan! That explains *everything!*" He ran toward Kiyoshi-chan, trying to say everything at once. *"Watashi wa Knuckleball desu. Namae wa nan desu ka? Hajimemashite!"*

"It explains nothing, Knucklehead," said Annie, shaking her head and walking up the street toward the two boys. They were already talking excitedly with each other, and taking turns trying on the goblin's head.

CHAPTER 4

A Little Hope for Little Harriet

"So," said Kiyoshi-chan's father, "you see that it isn't a head at all. It's a *helmet*."

"But it's more like a *mask* in front," said Knuckleball, straightening his glasses to see better. His baseball cap was off, and his hair was a sight. "And an ugly one at that. Looks like a *wild* man."

"You should see yourself, Knuckler," said Annie. "This guy looks *elegant* in comparison."

"It is very like the helmets of our ancient *samurai*," said Kiyoshi-chan's father. "Each warrior had his helmet made uniquely for himself, to terrify the enemy. The thing that you saw, whatever it was, was dressed and armed like an ancient Japanese warrior."

Annie and Knuckleball turned the object over in every direction, examining it inside and out. They were seated on the *tatami* of Kiyoshi-chan's home, around a low table, huddled in blankets. Kiyoshi-chan and his little sister Izumi-chan were also in the room, listening with puzzled smiles to the odd Japanese of these strange children. Kiyoshi-chan's mother came bustling in regularly, setting the table for breakfast.

"I like the dragon on top," said Knuckleball. "I especially like all those little tendrils round its mouth, like whiskers or earthworms. It's not so scary when you look at it up close."

"It's all such a mystery," said Annie. "I wonder if the rest of the armor was as empty as the helmet?"

"Of *course* not," said the father. "It was a tall costume, with a short person inside. What else could it have been?"

"I'm not sure," said Annie.

"Anyway," said Kiyoshi-chan's father, with a keen look at his guests, "we have some bigger mysteries than *that*."

The two children looked back at him, and smiled uncomfortably. The blue-gray light of a rain-filled morning was just becoming visible through a crack in the door.

"For one," said the man, "how do you speak Japanese, though you are American? Few Americans speak Japanese at all."

"Our father taught us," said Knuckleball.

"He's a professor of East Asian studies," said Annie. "At St. Gildas College. Near Boston. Do you know Boston?"

"Of course," said Kiyoshi-chan's father. "I must say that you speak our language very well."

Kiyoshi-chan could scarcely contain himself. "They talk as if they have cotton in their mouths," he said, grinning.

"Like cartoons," said Izumi-chan, giggling. "It makes my ears hurt to listen to them."

"You are rude," said their father.

"It's OK," said Annie. "I'm sure they're right."

"I have more questions," said the father. "Please tell me how you came here."

Annie and Knuckleball looked at each other.

"Here?" said Knuckleball. "Well, we walked."

"From where?" asked the father.

"From the train station," said Annie, too quickly.

Kiyoshi-chan's father sat up very straight and looked at them with a crooked smile.

"It's not far," said Annie. "It's just a few blocks away. It's a very nice train station, with a little garden on the platform."

"I know," said Kiyoshi-chan's father. "I use it every day. But you are hiding things from me. Where is your father? Where is your mother?"

"In America," said Annie and Knuckleball in unison.

"In Massachusetts," said Annie.

"And the two of you are here alone?"

There was a long pause.

"Well, not really *alone*," said Annie. "Not alone in a *completely* alone sort of way." This was even more confusing in Japanese than in English, and Kiyoshi-chan's father looked bothered. He waited, but the American children offered nothing else.

Kiyoshi-chan's mother brought in steaming bowls of rice and *miso* soup. The small room was full of the aroma.

"It is now eating," she said in English. "We have maximum hotness."

Kiyoshi-chan's father smiled at the children, continuing to speak in Japanese. "I am sorry I cannot speak English as well as my wife," he said. "She was always a much better student than I."

"Her English is wonderful," said Annie.

The mother laughed, holding her hand over her mouth. "Oh, no," she said. "Is not wonderful. Is very *peculiar* English."

The father was not concentrating on the conversation. His eyes seemed to be trying to dig deeply into the minds of the two American children, to uncover the mystery of their coming to his home.

"It is very strange," he said finally. "Very, very strange."

"I know," said Annie. "I'm sorry."

"*Sumimasen*," he said, "excuse me, but may I ask you one more question?"

"Of course," said Annie.

"Do you know anything," he asked, "about another American child near here? A little girl, about the size of Izumi-chan?"

Annie and Knuckleball scrambled to their feet, almost upsetting the table. "Yes!" said Annie. "Little Harriet! Have you seen her? Where? When?"

"I don't know if it was this Little Harriet," said the father. "But last night Kiyoshi-chan thinks he saw a little ghost in the form of a girl. Here."

"Where?!" said Annie. "Where?"

"In the garden," said the father. "In the darkest part of the night. But I am sorry."

"Why are you *sorry?*" cried Annie. "Tell us where she *went*."

"Now I am sorry that I mentioned it," said the father, very distressed. He looked almost as if he would cry. "It was so stupid of me. Please forgive me."

"Why?" insisted Annie, confused. "Why?"

"Because," said the father, "it could not have been this Little Harriet of yours. It must have been a dream of Kiyoshi-chan's."

"But why must it have been a dream?" asked Knuckleball. "I don't understand."

"Because of what Kiyoshi-chan said he saw," said the father. "He said that she came out of the garden like a ghost and dived back into the earth like a fish and *disappeared*."

He spread his hands out and rolled his eyes toward Kiyoshi-chan. "I'm so sorry for mentioning it. Kiyoshi-chan had a very difficult night of sleeping last night."

"But of *course* she dove into the ground!" said Knuckleball. "How else would she get away if she was scared?"

Kiyoshi-chan's father looked at the boy as if he had three heads.

"In America," he said, "do children swim through the ground like water? Do you learn how to do this in school?"

"Not in *school*," said Knuckleball. "Hardly."

Kiyoshi-chan's father slapped his knees decisively. "Your words make no sense," he said. "I don't think I want to listen anymore."

"The truth is stranger than you know," said Annie. "Give us time to tell you."

"Pah!" said the father, but not in a bad temper. "I think I have no time for your kind of truth."

"But look at the strange things you have seen already tonight," said Annie. "Look at this helmet."

"I've seen nothing," said Kiyoshi-chan's father. "Someone in a *samurai* costume played a prank on you in the street, and Kiyoshi-chan had another one of his foolish dreams. Last week he dreamed that the *yokozuna* Taiho was playing left field for the Boston Red Sox, in a pink kimono. Please let's eat. *Itadaki-masu.*"

"*Itadaki-masu*," said Annie and Knuckleball, but they looked at each other before picking up their chopsticks to eat. "She's here!" their eyes said to each other. And in the growing light of the blue-gray morning rain, it seemed to them as if it would be easy now to find her and bring her home again.

CHAPTER 5

Breaking and Entering

On the same rainy morning Annie and Knuckleball were eating breakfast with Kiyoshi-chan's family in Kashiwa, the yellow sun was rising on a stony mountain, a painted temple, and an old snow monkey in another part of Japan.

The mountain was covered with ancient, wind-shaped trees and overlooked a long valley that reached away to the horizon. In its history it had been climbed by untold numbers of pilgrims.

The temple was silent and philosophical, as temples should be, especially one famous for a seven-hundred-year-old garden.

The monkey was sitting under an alder tree, trying his best to look ignorant. His name was Basho, and he was an old macaque who possibly should have known better. Presently he was scratching his armpits, somersaulting, and trying to compose a *haiku* about a frog, three activities that very few humans can do simultaneously.

"White cherry blossoms," he said. "Falling dapple the old frog. The golden sun smiles."

"That is so *trite*," came a whisper from the bushes behind him. "At least try to be more original. I've read better haiku on cereal boxes."

"Bah," said Basho. "One flea on my rump has more

originality than you do in your whole soul. What could *you* know about haiku, *gaijin?*"

"And sit *still*," the voice whispered again. "Try not to make a scene. Do you have to flip like that every ten seconds?"

"Yes," said the monkey, standing on his head and looking between his legs at the temple. "Don't you?"

"No!" said the voice in the bushes. "Does the expression *self-control* mean anything at all to you?"

"Yes," the monkey replied again, doing a double flip in the air and landing on all fours. "It is no fun. It is one of the things that makes humans so boring. How can you stand it?"

"It comes in handy," said the voice. "When you have to do things like sneak into secret gardens for unnatural purposes. Do I have to tie you to the ground?"

"Try it," said the monkey. "You might be surprised who ends up in knots."

"Hmph," grumped the voice.

"Besides," said the monkey, "what do you think would be more conspicuous, a monkey acting just like a monkey, as I am, or a monkey just sitting still on the ground like a big dumb mushroom?"

The voice mumbled something reluctant, which Basho decided to interpret as an apology.

"Don't mention it," he said. He stood on his head, making a tripod with his two legs, and began to wave his bottom in the air. He peeped into the bushes and recited, "Age-old lotus pond. Suddenly a frog leaps in. Surprised water speaks."

"Oh, put a *sock* in it," said the voice, for the first time in English. "I'm *sick* of your haiku."

"*Domo arigato*," Basho said. "Your words are too kind. I don't understand your foreign gibberish exactly, but I sense that its meaning is that you *love* my poetry and will soon die if you don't hear more."

"Oh, go jump in an age-old pond yourself," said the voice.

The monkey kept up its vigil, watching the temple with one eye while leaping back and forth from the branches of the alder tree to the ground.

"Besides," said the monkey again, getting bored. Another haiku followed. "Roadside frog awaits. Eager to reach other side. Donkey steps on him."

"Well," said the invisible speaker, in a weary voice. "Now he's doing haiku about *roadkill*. Very sensitive. Sign of a great soul."

"I love poetry," said the monkey, spinning around like a top. "Helps my digestion."

At that moment, there was the sound of a quiet latch.

"Hark!" said Basho.

"Quiet!" hissed the voice.

The temple gate opened. A very, very old priest came out, closed the gate, and shuffled away up the mountain path, all bent over and tapping with his staff on the stones.

"Wow!" said a new voice in the bushes. "Did you see *him?* He must be at least a thousand years old."

"Is he the last one to leave?" asked the first voice.

"Should be," said the monkey. He waited till the old man had disappeared from sight, then scampered off toward the gate.

"C'mon, 'Siah," said the bodiless voice to someone, and out of the bushes came two more figures, running over the grass after the monkey. One of them was a teenaged boy, dressed in ragged, baggy clothes, who kept looking in all directions as he ran. The other was much smaller, a quick little boy of maybe five, whose feet hummed over the ground. In no time at all, the three of them had slipped inside the gate and shut it behind them.

"This is so ridiculous," said the bigger boy, as they made their way along a flagstoned path, looking in every direction as they went. He was a gentle bear of a young man, squarely built and soft-spoken, with handsome eyes. His head was covered with a fine dark stubble, like a Buddhist monk's. He had been named Owen Greatheart by his parents, and at some point had decided he wanted to be called by both his names. He had long ago forgotten why. "Why can't they just let people see their old garden without making us sneak around like criminals?"

"Yeah," said the little boy called 'Siah. "We're not gonna hurt it or anything." His face was the beautiful dark color of smooth chocolate, and his expressions were quick and bright. His name was properly Josiah, but no one called him that.

"Because," said the monkey, "they got tired of picking people's candy wrappers out of the philosophical shrubs." He got a poetic look on his monkey face for no good reason. "Young eager tadpole," he said. "Loses tail in the bright stream. The summer moon weeps."

"What is it with you and *frogs!*" said Owen Greatheart. "Your poetry is *irrelevant.*"

"Ah," said Basho the monkey, with infinite sadness. "You have no subtlety."

They came to a high fence made of tied bamboo stakes.

"Is this it?" said the big boy. There was a gate in the fence. Above the fence they could see the tops of small trees, but little else. They heard sparrows chittering inside, and the whisper of what might have been moving water. The three of them stood still suddenly, looking and listening. Something subtle shifted in the air.

"This is the place," said Owen Greatheart. "I can *tell*." He tried the latch of the gate. "There's no lock here."

"They trust us," Basho said with scorn, "not to try to enter where we're not wanted."

"Well," said Owen Greatheart, "we wouldn't if it weren't an emergency."

"Then *enter*," said the monkey, gesturing with exaggerated courtesy.

The big boy lifted the latch and they entered the ancient garden in cautious single file, with the monkey at the rear. Directly before them was a shaded corridor of trees, bending sharply to the right out of sight.

"Wait," said the monkey, hanging back. "I don't like this at all. Not another step until you give me a good reason for being here."

"Well," said Owen Greatheart, with patience. "Haven't we explained this before?"

"Not very clearly," said Basho. "We've hardly taken a spare breath since you kidnapped me."

"I'd hardly call it a *kidnapping*," said Owen Greatheart. "You told us about this garden and said you'd lead us to it."

"Ha!" said the monkey. "Only after you told me it was a matter of life and death. What could I say? Even a monkey has honor, you know."

"No, we don't," said 'Siah. "We didn't even know that monkeys do *poetry* till we met you."

"We *still* don't," said Owen Greatheart.

"Sorry," said the monkey. "Not another step without more information."

"OK," said Owen Greatheart, shutting the gate behind him and turning back to Basho. "Here goes, but let's make it quick. It all started in Boston."

"What is Boston?" asked the monkey.

"A city," said Owen Greatheart.

"In America," said 'Siah.

"What is America?" asked the monkey.

"Never *mind*," said Owen Greatheart, beginning to lose patience. "We'll give you the geography lesson next time. Anyway, there we were at the Museum of Fine Arts in Boston, in the Japanese garden."

"Ah!" said the monkey.

"It's just a little garden," said Owen Greatheart, "not old like this one, and you're supposed to stay on the path."

"Of *course*," said the monkey.

"So there we were," said Owen Greatheart, "looking at the little islands, the silver gravel, the bridges and lanterns, when Little Harriet suddenly saw a . . . I don't know the word in Japanese. A chipmunk."

"Does it have feathers?" asked Basho. "This *cheepu-mon-ku?*"

"No," said Owen Greatheart. "It's little, with stripes."

"It's fun," said 'Siah. "Which is why Little Harriet chased it."

"And Little Harriet is?" asked Basho.

"Our sister," said 'Siah. "She's only four, and real little. She didn't know any better."

"Well," said Owen Greatheart, "Little Harriet took off after that chipmunk and disappeared behind the stone lantern, into a thick clump of shrubs. We yelled at her first to come back, because we knew the museum would be mad at us if we all took off after her across the gravel, but she didn't seem to hear us."

"A child," said the monkey, "with a will of her own. And a great love of *cheepu-mon-ku*." He chuckled to himself, enchanted with his own pronunciation of the foreign word, and repeated it several times under his breath.

"That's what we thought," said Owen Greatheart, "but it's not really like Little Harriet. And that's when we felt the breeze."

"Are breezes unusual in Boston?" asked the monkey.

"No," said Owen Greatheart, "not at all. But this was a piney sort of breeze, like New Hampshire, and cool, blowing toward us from the place Little Harriet had disappeared. It was very hot and still in Boston that day."

"Ah," said Basho. "So what did you do?"

"Well, Annie went first," said Owen Greatheart. "She being the oldest. She tiptoed over, trying to step on stones and not on plants or the gravel. When she got there, she peeked behind the lantern and called for Little Harriet to come out. When she didn't, Annie went around behind the lantern herself, and seemed to take forever to come back."

"So did she?" asked Basho.

"Why, yes," said Owen Greatheart. "She poked her head back around with a funny look on her face and said that Little Harriet was *gone*. Well, that did something to all of us. It scared us terribly."

"We love Little Harriet," said 'Siah. "A lot."

"And the breeze was doing something to our heads, too, I think," said Owen Greatheart. "Anyway, before we knew it we all took off across the garden and ran behind the stone. I'm sure we left lots of footprints in the raked gravel. I feel bad about that."

"And?" said the monkey.

"And suddenly we weren't in Boston any more," said Owen Greatheart.

"And where were you?" asked the monkey.

"Well," said Owen Greatheart, but he didn't have a chance to finish. 'Siah clutched his arm.

"Owen!" said the little boy, looking over his shoulder toward the gate.

"What is it?" asked the monkey, still chuckling. "Another *cheepu-mon-ku?*" Then he also looked, and shrieked in terror.

There was a deep shout of anger, and before they had a chance even to turn around and prepare for the danger, a figure came leaping like a whirlwind through the gate, someone who seemed huge in a vast dark robe with a great cruel club in his hand.

"Look out!" cried Owen Greatheart, catching up to 'Siah and trying to shield him. "Run! Deeper into the garden!"

But before they could do it, the madman had leaped around them and cut them off on the path, clubbing them right and left until they were a bruised heap on the ground, 'Siah still under Owen Greatheart and protected from the heaviest blows. They cowered on the path, not daring to look up and see their enemy.

CHAPTER 6

Owen Greatheart Explains Things

"You are all very foolish," said a quavery, quiet voice.

The three conspirators still crouched cringing on the ground, waiting for another blow.

"Look up," said the voice.

"We don't dare," said Owen Greatheart. "We're afraid you'll hit us again."

"I haven't hit you yet," said the voice. "Why would I hit you now?"

"Tell that to my head," said Owen Greatheart.

"And to my poor sore bottom," said the monkey.

"Yeah," said 'Siah, not wanting to be left out. "Me too."

"No one has hit any of you," said the voice. "Go ahead, feel your heads and your poor sore bottoms. Are there any bruises? Any painful places?"

They did so, gingerly. It was true. Nothing was sore.

"You *expected* me to hit you," said the voice. "I frightened you, shouted a warning, and waved my old staff vigorously around your poor bodies until you collapsed, thinking you were beaten. Heh-heh. Was it a good trick?"

"Good trick," muttered Basho, but still no one dared look up.

"Look up, foolish creatures," said the voice. "I couldn't hurt a butterfly if my life depended on it. Or rather, I wouldn't."

Slowly the boys and monkey rolled apart from their heap on the ground. Standing above them, holding a short staff, was the ancient priest whom they had seen leaving the temple earlier. His face was thin and bony, crosshatched with wrinkles like a mystic map.

"We saw you leave," 'Siah said.

"And I saw you see me leave," said the old priest. "And you didn't see me return. These things happen. Do I truly look a thousand years old?"

"How did you hear that?" asked Owen Greatheart.

"With ears," said the old priest. "Now, stand up on your unbruised legs and walk quickly out of this garden."

"We can't," said Owen Greatheart.

"You must," said the old priest. "I'm not really giving you a choice."

"We have to go on," said Owen Greatheart. "Into the garden."

"Try," quavered the old priest, "and I shall have to wave my staff vigorously all around your bodies again." For some reason, this was daunting. The memory of those imaginary blows was somehow worse than if the bruises had been real. The three companions also realized, without saying so, that even if the old priest never actually touched them, his whirling staff would be as impassable as a wall.

'Siah looked like he would burst into tears. "But we don't even have any candy wrappers," he wailed. "We won't do any harm to your stupid old garden. We *never* litter, *anywhere.*"

The old priest squatted on the flagstone beside 'Siah and squinted at him.

"This seems to be an unreasonable emotion for just seeing a stupid old garden," he said. "You puzzle me."

"You don't understand," said Owen Greatheart. "We *have* to get into this garden, for the sake of someone else. We have to try to find something."

The old priest smiled. "That is the only reason to get into such a garden," he said. "To try to find Something. But you *also* don't understand. The reason I will not let you in is not for the sake of the garden. The garden can take care of itself. We don't fear your candy wrappers. The reason I will not let you in is for *your* sake."

"Is it because we're *foreigners?*" asked 'Siah. "Don't *you* start on this *gaijin* stuff. We get enough of that from this monkey."

"No," said the old priest, taking the little boy by the hand and leading him to a patch of soft moss. "Not because you are *gaijin*. In fact, in repayment for having greeted you with such a beating, I will now explain to you why this garden cannot be entered. Please be seated." He sat down, with his legs crossed lotus fashion and his back very straight. His hands were on his knees. The others imitated him. They could now hear the unmistakable sound of running water from beyond the trees. They waited for the old priest to speak.

"You have come," he said finally in an impressive tone, "to the Garden of a Thousand Worlds."

The two brothers looked at each other. "What does *that* mean?" asked 'Siah.

"Well," said the old priest. "Let me explain. Do you

know that a true Japanese garden is designed for philosophy as much as for beauty?"

"Yes," said Owen Greatheart. "We know that."

"Then you also may know that it is a place for *enlightenment*," said the old priest, "where an unexpected view may surprise you into a deep insight, a truth you've never known before."

"We know that," said Owen Greatheart. "We wanted to build one at home, a little one in our living room. That's why we were at the museum," he said, turning to Basho, "looking for ideas. It was for our dad's birthday."

The old priest chuckled. "A little one in your living room," he said, as if to himself. "A little one in your living room. These *gaijin*." He seemed more entertained than displeased by the idea. "So," he went on finally, after shaking his head for a while, "for you to have universal insights, your garden must be bigger than itself."

"Bigger than *itself?*" said 'Siah. "*Nothing's* that big. That's silly."

"No, it isn't, 'Siah," said Owen Greatheart. "I get what he means. A stone can represent a mountain, a little pagoda can be a temple, a bed of white gravel can be a river, or the sea. Each small thing *means* more than it looks."

The old priest looked at Owen Greatheart. "Good," he said. "*Very* good."

"But so *what?*" said Owen Greatheart. "There are gardens everywhere made according to this philosophy. Why can't we see *this* one?"

The old priest paused.

"It's just another philosophical garden," persisted Owen. "Please? *Onegai-shimasu?*"

The old man sat very still, as if deep in thought. Flies buzzed, while invisible birds chirped and beeped, rustling the foliage. The monkey rolled several somersaults in the pathway, ending up seated rightwise and scratching his scalp with a shrewd squint.

"This Garden," the old priest finally continued, as if there had been no pause, "is not like other gardens."

Owen Greatheart rolled his eyes. "Everyone says that about their *own* garden," he said.

"Other philosophical gardens simply *represent* the Universe," said the old priest, ignoring the comment. "And so in a sense are also gardens of a thousand worlds. But in this Garden, the whole Universe is truly *contained*."

"I don't understand," said Owen Greatheart.

"*Everywhere*," said the old priest, "is here. *Here* you find every Place that *is*."

"So it *is* a gateway!" said Owen Greatheart. "We *can* go through here to find Little Harriet. That's what we *want*."

The old priest looked at him. "Oh, it's a gateway all right," he said. His voice sounded regretful.

"Perfect!" said 'Siah.

"Don't you see what that means, foolish children?" asked the old priest. "There are infinite places *in* this Garden. When you enter, *you do not know where it will take you*."

"*Cool*," said 'Siah.

"*Not* cool," said the old priest. "The possibilities are *endless*. It could take you to New Delhi or Philadelphia, Mars or Mercury, Heaven or Hell. It could take you to the Andromeda Galaxy, or to another universe altogether. How do you know if it will take you to this Little Harriet of yours? It could take you inside one of the cells of that lizard on that tree. Would you enjoy that, little boy?" he asked 'Siah.

"Sure!" said 'Siah, looking eagerly at the bright blue lizard.

"Bah! There's *more*," said the old priest, now annoyed, but obviously calling up all his inner disciplines to hide it. "Once you get wherever you get, then how do you get back? No one has ever returned out of this Garden. There are fairy tales of some who returned, bringing glories or horrors from some other world. But the *true* tales are of the ones who were lost forever. You go in *and you never return*."

"But we don't *want* to come back here," said 'Siah. "Once we find Little Harriet, we just want to go *home*. That's OK if we can't get back here. No *offense*."

"What makes you think you can find your way *home* from that lizard cell, or from Alpha Centauri?" asked the old priest. "What has given you the impression that you can *choose* your destination from this Garden at all, even to find Little Harriet?"

"Well," said Owen Greatheart, staring hard at the old priest, "we *are* experienced at this. We've been traveling through garden gateways for *days*. That's how we came from Boston to here. And we've been able to stay right on Little Harriet's trail, right up till the last time."

"So?" said the old priest.

"So," faltered Owen Greatheart. "Well, I've just assumed that we'd be able to do the same thing again. However we did it before."

"And how was *that*?" said the old priest. "*Think!*

You are making the mistake of judging this Garden by all the other ones you've seen. But even consider *them*. So far you've only been traveling the local train lines, so to speak, from one little stop to the next, and you must confess that you have no real idea how you got here. And *this*, my friends, isn't just another little train station. This is Haneda International Airport, or maybe Cape Canaveral, *with no return flights*."

Despair overwhelmed Owen Greatheart, as he realized how little he knew about what he was doing. *What were they doing here?* He covered his eyes, feeling weary.

"I don't think you really *know*," said 'Siah to the old priest. "Have you ever actually been in this garden?"

"No," said the old priest, smiling. "Not beyond this bend."

"How can I ask this in polite Japanese?" said Owen Greatheart, looking up again. "How do we know that you're not just an old fraud? We know so *many* priests."

The old priest merely smiled, and answered the wrong question. "There is no way to ask that question in polite Japanese," he said. "Now, tell me your story. Why are you here? Maybe it will help us all understand."

Owen Greatheart sighed. "Well, maybe it will," he said, without conviction. He considered a moment, and began. "It's like this. We are seven brothers and sisters, and we live near Boston, Massachusetts."

So he told the story, just as he had started to do earlier with Basho the monkey. He told of the museum garden and Little Harriet's chipmunk, how all of them had rushed behind the lantern and found themselves in some indescribable sense being swallowed up by the garden, then ending up to their amazement in a small walled garden in an unknown country, with no Little Harriet in sight.

"And then what?" asked the monkey.

"We ran out of that garden," said Owen Greatheart. "There was no one around. It was hot and sunny, and there was a dusty country road running by. We could smell wood smoke and cooking food, but everyone must have been working in the fields. We ran all around the garden and the house it was attached to, but there was no sign of Little Harriet. There was a sound like really faraway thunder in the distance, way up the road. We ran in that direction and could see what looked like a cloud of dust way far away, like might be behind a big truck on a dirt road. Then Q.J. found something."

"Q.J. is another brother?" asked the old priest.

"A sister," said Owen Greatheart. "She's thirteen."

"We call her Quiddity Jane," said 'Siah. "It's a private joke."

"What did she find?" asked the monkey. "Tell the story, tell the story."

"One of Little Harriet's sneakers," said Owen Greatheart. "From that we knew she had gone that way, so we started to run. Somehow we knew that she was in that cloud of dust."

"Somehow I know it also," said the monkey. He frowned. "I think I begin to see a certain *hand* in this."

"Hush, monkey," said the old priest.

"We walked and ran forever, it seemed like," said Owen Greatheart. "Like in a dream. We got so tired that our legs were like rubber, but we didn't seem to need food or sleep. Something strange happens when you travel the garden gateways. The time doesn't seem to make any sense. That time, days and nights seemed to pass, but some of the days seemed to last forever, and other ones only seemed to be an hour from sunrise to sunset. We began to see people now and then, villages sometimes and workers in the rice paddies, but we ran on and on and on, and that cloud of dust never seemed to get either closer or farther away. Until after about ten or eleven of those strange days, the thunder stopped and there was no dust cloud ahead anymore."

"He was waiting for you," said the old priest.

"Yes," said Owen Greatheart. "We stopped running and began to walk on more cautiously, wondering if it made sense to sneak up on whatever or whoever had Little Harriet. But then we came over a rise at last, and there we saw him standing in the middle of the road, directly in front of a great gate, a *torii*. He had Little Harriet in a sack over his shoulder, with just her head sticking out. We couldn't tell if she was dead or alive or unconscious or anything."

"*Oni*," said the monkey. "A demon warrior. I knew it."

"I guess," said Owen Greatheart. "His armor was red and blue with gold designs all over it, and his helmet had a leaping lion on the top. His mask was black like coal with a huge bushy mustache under the nose and a ferocious gaping mouth. He was gigantic, as tall as two of me. He laughed at us."

He fell silent. The old priest watched him. Even the monkey said nothing.

"Then he smote us with some kind of power," said

Owen Greatheart. "He waved his sword at us and it was like a blast of fire so we couldn't stand up. I think it knocked us out, because when we looked again he was gone. With Little Harriet."

"But the great gate, by the road," said the old priest. "There was another garden there, inside?"

"Yes, yes," said Owen Greatheart. "Of course. We went in the gate and once again felt that cool mountain breeze. We followed it to a garden, one with a waterfall and red maples. We knew he must have gone that way. We walked around the garden until we found the source of the breeze, a bamboo grove in the deep corner. All we had to do was walk in and we found ourselves in another place entirely, a little courtyard garden in a city of some kind."

"The next train stop," said the old priest.

"Yes," said Owen Greatheart.

"Excuse me," said 'Siah, nervously. No one paid him any attention.

"Then," said the old priest, "how did it go the next time? Did you run like the wind and find him just disappearing into the next garden gateway, with a mocking laugh over his shoulder?"

"Something like that," said Owen Greatheart.

"And every other time also?" asked the old priest.

"Yes," said Owen Greatheart. He stared at the ground between his feet.

"Do you not see how you have gotten here?" asked the old priest. "Was it your mastery of the gardens that kept you so long on the track of your Little Harriet?"

"No," admitted Owen Greatheart at last, still not lifting his eyes. "He lured us. The demon never really let himself get out of sight. He *wanted* us on his track, for some reason." *Why?* he wondered, completely befuddled. *Why? Why any of this?*

"Giving you the illusion," said the old priest, "that *you* were somehow in control of where you were going."

"Yes," said Owen Greatheart. "I see, of course, that we're hopelessly lost. But this garden is *still* our only hope. It's the only known gateway we have, and it's a powerful one. And if the demon warrior wanted us on his trail this far, won't he maybe use this garden to get us back on it again?"

"You assume," began the old priest, "that . . ."

"Excuse me!" said 'Siah again, louder.

"What's the *matter,* 'Siah?" asked Owen Greatheart. "Do you have to go to the bathroom *again?*"

"*No,*" said the little boy in a trembly voice. "I was just wondering. Should that big mound of moss be *moving* like that?"

CHAPTER 7

Sumo Lessons

Meanwhile, Kiyoshi-chan was having the time of his life. It was Saturday afternoon, and he had taken Knuckleball to school with him that morning. His teacher Takashima-sensei had trouble keeping other students focused on their work with the strange *gaijin* boy in the back of the classroom. They kept swarming around Knuckleball all day, touching his yellow hair and laughing as if he were an especially clever animal in the zoo. They ooo'd when he took a bite of cookie and aahh'd when he drank his milk, and then kept asking him for his autograph on their school notebooks. Knuckleball pulled his battered cap down over his eyes as if to hide from his celebrity status, but Kiyoshi-chan couldn't help reveling in this new glory, added on to his great sumo victory earlier in the week.

But the real fun came in the afternoon, when the two boys ran up the walled street and into Kiyoshi-chan's yard for a whole half-day of freedom. It had taken almost no time for them to discover that they were friends, and they had already found many points of common interest. Kiyoshi-chan had borrowed a Knuckleball-sized baseball glove from one of his friends and they had already played an endless game of catch in the tiny yard, counting in Japanese up to six hundred forty-six catches without a miss and having to start over.

"On Sunday," Kiyoshi-chan said afterward, "we will play baseball with my friends, at the school ground."

Now, though, on Saturday afternoon, the game was sumo. They drew a ring in the smooth-swept dirt of the yard, and then the lessons began. First, Kiyoshi-chan tried to teach Knuckleball the differences among the seventy *kimari-te*, or proper winning techniques, of sumo.

"Techniques? I thought it was just two big blobs running into each other, like in football," Knuckleball said. For him, baseball was the only true sport on earth.

Kiyoshi-chan laughed, and taught him *yorikiri*, and *uwatenage*, and *kawazugake*, and *uchimuso*, and *yobimodoshi*, and *hatakikomi*. He taught him the advantage of *sukuinage*, which is done from an inside gripping position, over *tsukiotoshi*, which is done from outside. He taught him the difference between *oshidashi*, *tsukidashi*, *waridashi*, and *okuridashi*.

"Can't I just make up my own way?" Knuckleball asked. "Some of my own *kimari-te?*" Somehow he couldn't get Kiyoshi-chan to understand the question. There seemed to be seventy *kimari-te* and only seventy. When Knuckleball repeated the question, Kiyoshi-chan was still bewildered, so Knuckleball tried to demonstrate.

"What if I just do this?" he asked, faking one way with his head, sidestepping, and pushing Kiyoshi-chan out from behind.

Kiyoshi-chan stood with his hands on his hips, looking hurt. "That is *tricky* sumo," he said. "Tricky sumo is not good sumo. It is not worthy of a true *yokozuna*."

"That's *weird*," said Knuckleball. "In basketball we trick people all the time. It's called faking the guy out of his sneakers."

"This is not basketball," said Kiyoshi-chan, offended now. "This is *sumo*."

"Wow," said Knuckleball, laughing. "Can't you even compromise a little? Let's just have some fun with *tricky* sumo."

"No!" said Kiyoshi-chan.

Knuckleball shrugged, realizing that Kiyoshi-chan was serious. "OK," he said. "Sorry. Teach me more."

So Kiyoshi-chan taught Knuckleball to do *tsuri-dashi*, which is when a wrestler lifts the other up by his great belt and sets him down outside the ring. To demonstrate, Kiyoshi-chan managed to lift Knuckleball up an inch or two off the ground by his belt loops and wobble over to the edge of the ring. Knuckleball whooped and wrapped his legs around Kiyoshi-chan's so he couldn't be put down. They wavered there, swaying with laughter, until they both finally collapsed in a giggling heap.

"Whoo-boy," said Knuckleball, picking up his glasses and putting them back on. They were so bent by now that they made his whole face look lopsided. "Ouch. I'm gonna have to call that a *wedgie-dashi*."

"What is *wedgie?*" asked Kiyoshi-chan.

"Never mind," said Knuckleball. "What's next?"

But after three or four more *kimari-te*, Knuckleball threw himself down on the doorstep of the house.

"I can't remember all of these," he said, laughing. "Can't we just *sumo?*"

Still Kiyoshi-chan was firm. "You must learn it *properly*," he said. "Let me just teach you one more thing. Without this we can't sumo at all."

But this one thing was the hardest of all. He tried to

teach him the proper way to do the *tachi-ai*, the first great charge of the wrestlers.

"First you squat down," he said, "like this."

They did so, sitting on their haunches with their backs straight and their hands on their knees.

"OK," said Knuckleball. "That's easy. Now who says Go?"

"No one says Go," said Kiyoshi-chan.

"Oh, *you* can," said Knuckleball, misunderstanding. "I don't care who says Go. Or Annie will come out and say Go for us. Hey, Annie!"

"No one says Go," said Kiyoshi-chan.

The door slid open and Annie stepped out. "What's up, Knuckler?" she asked. "I'm helping with dinner." There was the smell of meat and other things cooking, a special meal of *katsu-donburi* for the two foreign guests.

"No one says Go," said Kiyoshi-chan, for the third time.

"What do you mean, no one says Go?" said Knuckleball to Kiyoshi-chan. Annie waited, sensing something between the two friends.

"No one does," said Kiyoshi-chan. "The two *rikishi* must harmonize their readiness together. They must both sense when the other is ready to fight, and after they both touch their fists to the ground, they begin."

"No one blows a whistle?" asked Knuckleball.

"No," said Kiyoshi-chan.

"No gun, or buzzer?" asked Knuckleball. "Doesn't the referee stamp his foot, or clap his hands, or yell, or *something*?"

"No," said Kiyoshi-chan. "True sumo wrestlers are

able to know the proper moment. Without this, you cannot be a true sumo wrestler."

Knuckleball hesitated. "But," he said, "we *aren't* true sumo wrestlers. We're just two kids sumo wrestling in your backyard. Can't Annie just say Go *this* time?"

"No, please," said Kiyoshi-chan. "When I sumo, I am no longer Kiyoshi-chan. I am Taiho himself."

"So who's Taiho?" asked Knuckleball. "I've never heard of him." Annie shrugged and turned to go back into the house.

"Of course not," said Kiyoshi-chan. "Americans know nothing of sumo."

"That's not *true*," said Knuckleball. "I watch sumo on TV and check it online lots of times when there's a tournament going. I like Akebono, the *yokozuna*. He's about seven feet tall and weighs a ton. And two other *yokozuna* are Taka-somebody and his brother Waka-somebody. I can't remember their whole names. And Musashimaru is almost a *yokozuna*. So there."

Kiyoshi-chan looked sideways at Knuckleball, wondering if he was joking. "There is no Akebono," he said. "Or Taka-Waka-somebody. Only Taiho and Kashiwado."

Annie turned slowly back from the door, unable to break away from the conversation. A vague disquiet stirred somewhere inside her. She sat down on the doorstep to listen.

Knuckleball stared at Kiyoshi-chan. "That's strange," he said. "I guess I was confused. Sorry."

But Kiyoshi-chan was upset. He was upset at himself for spoiling this afternoon with his passion for the dignity of sumo, and he was upset with Knuckleball for not caring about the spirit of a true sumo wrestler. Maybe no foreigner could be a true *rikishi*, but Knuckleball didn't seem like a *gaijin*, he seemed like a brother.

"Listen, Knuckleball," he said. He had trouble with this nickname, which came out with a couple of extra syllables, no matter how hard he tried. *Na-ku-ru-ba-ru.* "Try to understand. What if the great *Yazu* of the Boston Red Sox tried to play left field with a glove this big?" He stretched his arms out to their fullest extent. "Would you think he was playing with the spirit of a true baseball player?"

Knuckleball tilted his head as if to look at his friend from a new angle.

"Well?" said Kiyoshi-chan.

"Who is *Yazu?*" asked Knuckleball.

"Who is *Yazu?*" cried Kiyoshi-chan. "How can you say who is *Yazu?*"

Knuckleball shrugged, avoiding Kiyoshi-chan's eyes. He didn't know how to escape this conversation. "I've never heard of *Yazu,*" he said.

Kiyoshi-chan stared at Knuckleball, dumbfounded. "Didn't you say you came from Boston?" he said. "Didn't you say how you love baseball?"

"Yes," said Knuckleball. "And yes."

"Haven't you been to *Fenway Park?*" shouted Kiyoshi-chan. He said the name with a sort of passionate reverence, as if it were a temple or a sacred mountain like Fuji-*sama*.

"Yes," said Knuckleball. "Twice last season. And I watch the Red Sox all the time on TV."

Kiyoshi-chan clutched his head. "Then how

can you say who is *Yazu?*" he cried again. "Do you know who is *To-nee See?* Do you know who is *Jee-mu Ro-nu-bu-ru-gu?*"

Knuckleball shook his head, as distressed as his friend. "I'm sorry, Kiyoshi-chan," he said. "I can't even begin to guess what those names are."

Kiyoshi-chan took a deep breath, trying not to be angry. "Tell me then, Oh Person From Boston Who Loves Baseball," he said. "Who plays for *your* Boston Red Sox?"

Knuckleball sighed. "Well," he said. "There's Manny Ramirez, and Nomar Garciaparra, and Pedro Martinez. Nomar's my favorite. He plays shortstop. And Tim Wakefield throws a knuckler, like me."

Annie was listening with her head down.

Kiyoshi-chan scrutinized the face of his friend. "*No-ma-ru?*" he said carefully. "I have never heard of Nomaru. What happened to *Ree-ko?*" He hesitated. "Knuckleball. Who plays left field for the Boston Red Sox? Is it not the great *Yazu?*"

"No," said Knuckleball. "They're having trouble in left field now because Manny's been hurt. Lots of times it's Troy O'Leary or other people. Nobody regular."

Kiyoshi-chan shook his head in complete confusion. "You are making fun of me, Knuckleball. Why are you doing this? Aren't we friends?"

Knuckleball looked at Annie, but knew she would be no help. Her only sport passion was actually *playing* soccer. She despised the whole concept of *watching* sports at all ("Unless people come to see *you*," Knuckleball often said to her. "You don't mind that, now do you?"), and had no idea whether the Red Sox played baseball, football, or hockey. He was amazed to see that her face had gone pinched and strange, as if she had seen another demon.

"Annie!" he said. "Are you gonna throw up?"

She reached out for him from her sitting position, so he stood in front of her and let her put her head on his shoulder. He hoped she wouldn't throw up all over him.

"I think we're in trouble, Knuckler," said Annie in a thin voice, as if from far away.

He pulled back to see her better. "Trouble?" he asked. "What kind of trouble?"

"I don't know exactly," she said. "But maybe terrible trouble. If I'm right, I don't know how we'll ever get home again."

He jerked away from her. "What do you mean!" he cried. "What do you mean never get home again?"

"I don't know," she said. "I shouldn't have said anything till I know. We need Owen right now. He's the sports fiend. He would know for sure. But Knucklehead, I'm afraid."

Knuckleball got a sudden picture in his mind of his dad and mom waiting for them at home, wondering where their children had gone. His eyes stung with tears, but he rubbed them before Kiyoshi-chan could see.

"That's ridiculous, Annie," he said, and putting his head down on her shoulder, he began to cry.

CHAPTER 8

The Way Out

In a very very dark place, two sisters sat side by side, holding each other. Moments before they had stood with four other brothers and sisters in bright sunshine, and for the umpteenth time had taken a deep breath of evergreen breeze and plunged into a garden place that they believed would keep them on the trail of lost Little Harriet.

But something had gone wrong. In that particular garden, the breeze had been flowing outward from a fiery cluster of azaleas growing on a small stone island. As they plunged into the flowers, they had expected the familiar sensation of the ground dropping out from under them, or of the garden rushing upward to receive them. But this time there seemed to be a resistance of some kind. They started to sink into the ground, but before they disappeared beyond their waists, the ground suddenly solidified again, and they were trapped. The shortest ones had been in the greatest danger, because what was waist-high for the others could have smothered them. Fortunately, 'Siah was perched on Owen Greatheart's shoulders, but six-year-old Libby was buried up to her chin, and she looked around for help, with wild eyes.

"Q.J.!" she had cried out, and her sister leaned over to soothe her. So when the bottom fell away from them this time, Q.J. and Libby were together, and they clutched each other and wailed in unison as they plummeted into space.

The passage to the next garden had been horrible this time. Where it had always before been a dreamy, swirling sort of float into the next place, over in a few seconds, this time was full of turbulence, faraway voices, disturbing shapes, and ugly shouts. Still holding to each other, Libby and Q.J. tumbled through clouds and darkness, breathless with fear. When they at last crawled through the next gateway, shaken and disheveled, they found themselves in total darkness.

"Do you think we're blind?" asked Libby. "I'm holding my hand right in front of my face and I can't see a thing."

Q.J. was always logical. "Relax, Squib. There's not much chance of *both* of us going blind at exactly the same time. I think it's just *dark*."

"Real dark," said Libby. "Really, *really* dark."

At first it was more interesting than frightening, because neither of them had ever known such complete darkness before. Once Q.J. had tried to entertain her smaller siblings by seeing how dark she could make one bedroom in broad daylight. They had covered the skylight and windows and every possible crack, but somehow enough light managed to seep in so that when their eyes adjusted to it, they could still see the faint shapes of things. They had not come up with any solid explanation for this, though Knuckleball as usual had several exotic ideas, one of them involving hypnosis by aliens.

"Maybe our eyes will get used to this," said Libby. "Then we'll be able to see something."

"Maybe," said Q.J. "But I think they've had enough time to adjust. And I *still* can't see anything."

"It must be real, real midnight then," said Libby. "Maybe it'll start to get light soon."

"Maybe," said Q.J.

They huddled together, afraid to venture away from the place where they were sitting. The surface under them seemed to be sharp-edged gravel, but by shifting around they were able to get a little comfortable in each other's arms.

"If it's nighttime," said Libby, "we should sleep."

"So sleep," said Q.J. "Want me to rock you?"

"Yes, please," said Libby. She was, after all, only six. "I wonder where the others are? Why did we get all blown apart like that?"

"I don't know," said Q.J. "I don't know why it was so different this time. Maybe there was no reason. There aren't always reasons for things." She pulled Libby onto her lap, and sang her some songs to help her sleep, small melodies that she sang over and over until the little girl slumped into a sound sleep. Then the long hours began to pass for Q.J. After a while, her back started to hurt and the gravel underneath her became increasingly painful. The air was cold, not bitter but uncomfortable, and very still. She would not do anything to wake Libby, so Q.J. sat as motionless as she could, trying to relax every muscle in her body to help it hurt less.

She woke up suddenly, out of a terrifying dream. She had been dreaming that they were all together again on a little stone island in the ocean, a little stone island with a thick cluster of bright red azaleas. It was dark and stormy, and the waves were crashing on their island. Then they had seen Little Harriet, riding a dark storm cloud over the ocean, waving to them and laughing as if she were riding the carousel at Canobie Lake Park. They called out to her, but she laughed some more and her face was actually shining, as if it were the only thing in that whole abyss of wind and water that was in sunlight. Then the storm cloud she was riding on turned into a dragon, a vast bronze unthinkable creature writhing from one horizon to the other, and she laughed some more. The dragon disappeared with a pop and Little Harriet's tiny white body was falling falling falling through the clouds toward the black ocean, still looking toward them laughing with that sunny face. Then Q.J. woke up, with a dark, hollow certainty that Little Harriet was dead.

"What a ridiculous thing to think," she said to herself, always logical. "A stupid dream doesn't mean anything." But she couldn't shake away the thought. She pinched herself to try to get a little more sense. Libby must have been ready to awake, because that small movement made her sit up, stretching and yawning. Q.J. felt the breath of her yawns on her cheek.

"Cover your mouth when you yawn, Squibber," she said, teasing, trying to protect her little sister from the darkness inside her, which seemed to have become deeper than the darkness outside. "Rude person."

Libby giggled. Then Q.J. felt the little girl cuddle herself with her arms against the cold. "It's still dark," Libby said. "Really dark."

"Yes," said Q.J.

"Why doesn't morning come?" asked Libby.

"We must be in a place," said Q.J., "where morning doesn't come."

"There's no such place," said Libby.

Q.J. gave no answer to this.

"If only we had a *flashlight*," said Libby. "In stories, people always happen to have just the things they need, like matches or rope or something. Why can't we be in a story?"

Q.J. hit herself in the forehead with the palm of her hand, and groaned.

"What did you just do?" asked Libby. "Did you just hit yourself?"

Q.J. gave no answer, but grabbed her backpack and zipped it fiercely open.

"I'm such a total idiot," she said.

"What!" asked Libby. "Don't tell me you've had a flashlight this whole time."

"All right," said Q.J. "I won't tell you that."

"Have you?" asked Libby. "Have you had a flashlight this whole entire time?"

"Not exactly," said Q.J., but a sudden beam of white light shot out from her hand. She laughed. "My reading light," she said. "The one that clips onto books for reading in bed. I got it for Christmas."

"Well, you goose," said Libby. "Why didn't you remember it before?"

"Who knows?" said Q.J. "Memories are funny things."

She pointed the beam outward, moving it in a semicircle around her body.

"It's a *cave*," said Libby.

"A mine, I think," said Q.J. "Not a natural cave,

anyway. Look at the tool marks on the walls and ceiling. This is a tunnel, carved out by people."

"But where's the garden?" asked Libby. "I thought we had figured out that we were traveling from garden to garden."

Q.J. swung the beam behind them, in the direction from which they had first come. She gasped. "Look!" she said, in wonder.

They were facing the dead end of the tunnel, a wall of black stone. But between them and the wall was a thing of beauty, a tiny garden all of stone. There was a delicate waterfall of white gravel, and a pond of the same. There were two stones, one vertical and one tortoise-shaped, set up near one end of the pond, the tallest one only up to Libby's waist. Trees were represented by some natural stone formations, twisted intricate shapes brought to this cavern from some place that had weather and flowing water. There was a stubby stone lantern among the trees.

"It looks so real," said Libby. "It's beautiful."

"It *is* real," said Q.J. "It's as real as anything can be." And for a moment there was something about the low bright light and shifting shadows that made the little garden seem like a landscape in early morning, somebody's homeland, with animals beginning to move behind the trees and a village of living, waking people just over that ridge, between those two great pines. . . . Q.J. had to shake herself.

"Look at the char on the lantern," she said. "It's been lit before. Maybe a long time ago."

"Who do you think made it?" asked Libby.

"Who can say?" said Q.J. again. "This looks like an

abandoned mine, and maybe some miner once tried to make it a little more beautiful."

"Even though no one else would see it," said Libby. "I wish I could meet him."

They continued to examine the tiny garden, entranced, until finally sensible Q.J. sat back on her heels.

"It's stupid to keep wasting the batteries," she said. "We have to get out of here."

"Let's go," said Libby. "Out must be *that* way."

The tunnel was not perfectly straight, but it had the advantage of having no branches or side passages. There was no choice but one, so the two sisters were able to move quickly along it holding hands. The footing was good and smooth. Before long they began to hear a sound.

"Water," said Q.J. "Maybe a stream of some kind."

And indeed around the bend they came upon a small trickle of a stream so unexpectedly that Libby put her foot in it before she could stop.

"Yuck," she said. "I hate wet socks."

"Tough," said Q.J. "They'll dry."

On they went, over the stream and along the tunnel, toward a sharp bend that concealed what was beyond it.

"I have a feeling," said Libby, "that we're gonna see something *good* around that next bend."

Q.J. laughed in spite of herself. "Like maybe our front door?" she said. "Or at least a telephone?"

"Maybe," said Libby. "Or maybe Daddy. Or Mummy." She laughed. Since seeing the stone garden, anything seemed possible, and that bend ahead seemed full of magic chances. They were almost running when they finally reached it.

"Here we go!" cried Libby, and they ran around the bend, hand in hand. They thudded to a stop against another black wall of stone.

"A dead end!" wailed Libby. "A dead end!"

"It can't be," Q.J. said, arguing with her own eyes. "Both ends of the tunnel can't be a dead end. It's *impossible*."

"It's impossible," said Libby, fighting back the tears. "But it *is*."

CHAPTER 9

Weaving a Net of Words

"Now listen," said Annie. She was squatting on her heels in front of the garden of Kiyoshi-chan's family. Knuckleball and Kiyoshi-chan were on each side of her, in the same position. There was the pungent aroma of cooking *soba* coming from the kitchen window, where the head of Kiyoshi-chan's mother, wrapped in a blue print kerchief, was visible. It was finally no longer raining over Kashiwa, and there were even bits of blue sky overhead.

"Now listen," said Annie again. "We need to go about this more *scientifically*. We've been wasting too much time."

"Go about what?" asked Knuckleball.

"Go about gathering everyone together again," said Annie, "and finding Little Harriet, and getting back home again."

"Oh," said Knuckleball. "Is that all? Piece of cake."

He said "piece of cake" in literal Japanese, just like the rest of the conversation, which confused Kiyoshi-chan a lot. It took a while to explain the expression to his satisfaction, and even then he wore a puzzled look afterward.

"Especially," said Annie, "we need to figure out everything we can about these garden passageways we've been using. There must be some rational, scientific explanation for them. If we can only figure them out better, maybe we can learn how to *control* them."

"That would help," said Knuckleball. "So far they've just been dumping us places, but at least they've kept us on the track of Little Harriet. This last time was weird, though. It almost killed us all."

"Oh, don't exaggerate, Knuckleball," said Annie. "It was just uncomfortable for a second, like somebody was trying to keep it shut. Or like we were too late, trying to squeeze through a closing door. Who knows?" She shrugged.

"Yeah," said Knuckleball, "but then it blew us all in different directions. Who knows where the others are now?"

"Exactly why we need to approach this more systematically," said Annie. "Now, let's put together everything we know so far about this . . . this . . . means of transportation."

"OK," said Knuckleball. He straightened his glasses, as he always did when he was about to act like a professor. "We know that it gets us places in a hurry," he said, "even halfway around the world."

"Right," said Annie. "Distances seem to mean nothing to it. And neither does . . ." She stopped without finishing her sentence.

"And neither does what?" asked Kiyoshi-chan.

"Never mind for now," said Annie. "I'll tell you when I find out for sure. So what else do we know?"

"Well," said Knuckleball, "we know that not *all* Japanese gardens are gateways from one place to another. We've tried plenty just in the past few days that didn't get us anything but facefuls of shrubbery."

"Actually," said Annie. "We don't even really know if *only* Japanese gardens are gateways. Maybe other gardens would also serve as gateways."

"Do people in other countries make such gardens?" asked Kiyoshi-chan. "Gardens that are supposed to be bigger on the inside than they are on the outside?"

"I don't know," said Annie. "I never really thought about it. I don't think most people in other countries *have* a philosophy of gardening, like the Japanese do. Most people just garden according to what seems nicest to look at."

Kiyoshi-chan's old *obaa-san* poked her white head out the door and looked with friendly curiosity at the children in the yard. Moving very slowly, she slid the door shut and shuffled down off the porch toward them. The children stood up and bowed to her, as she smiled and bobbed at them. Her face was as wrinkled as a dried peach. She moved away, pottering meaninglessly.

"She's very beautiful," said Annie.

Kiyoshi-chan gaped at her. "Beautiful?" he said. "How can you call my grandmother *beautiful?* Did you use the wrong word?"

"No," said Annie. "I used just the right word. She is more beautiful than almost anyone I ever saw. I can't explain why exactly. In some people the years add up differently than in others. You can see at one look how *hard* she's had to work all her life, but there's no sourness in her at all."

"It's true that she's had a hard life," said Kiyoshi-chan. "So many wars. She had an older brother who died fighting the Russians."

"The Russians?" said Knuckleball. "I don't picture

the Japanese fighting the Russians. You mean in World War II?"

"No," said Kiyoshi-chan. "I mean in the *old* war with the Russians."

Annie looked at Knuckleball, who was puzzled. "Nineteen-oh-four, Knuckler," she said, then wished she hadn't, as she saw him look hard at the old woman again.

"No *way*," he said. "She's not *that* old."

"Well," said Annie, quickly, "back to the gardens. What else do we know?"

"We know we can't go back the way we've come," said Knuckleball. "The gateways seem to close up as soon as we come out of them."

"Do we know that for sure?" asked Annie. "Have we really tried it? Why, Kiyoshi-chan saw Little Harriet come right out of this garden and then dive right back in."

"That's true," said Knuckleball. "I didn't even *think* of that. I hate when I don't think of things."

"Maybe I dreamed it," said Kiyoshi-chan.

"What else do we know?" asked Annie. "Think *hard*."

They squatted on their heels and thought hard, while Kiyoshi-chan watched them. Brown house sparrows hopped around the branches of a budding cherry tree over their heads. Knuckleball took off his glasses and rubbed his eyes to concentrate, while Annie stared at a particular knot in the twine that tied the bamboo fence together.

"Nothing," admitted Knuckleball at last. "We know nothing else. We've just been blindly stumbling our way along after Little Harriet. We can't possibly figure out how to control these gardens, or to choose where we go. They take us wherever they want. And so far they've wanted to take us wherever Little Harriet went."

"Until last time," said Annie. "Then only two of us, and now *we've* lost her. I thought this garden might be the key, but if it's a gateway it's obviously closed." She stood up and stamped her foot on the very spot where Kiyoshi-chan said he had seen Little Harriet dive into the earth. A little cloud of dust poofed out around her shoe.

"Listen," said Knuckleball. "Maybe it has something to do with the person, not the garden. Maybe there's something about *Little Harriet* that opens the passages between gardens. She was the first one to have a garden open up to her, there in Boston."

"Maybe," agreed Annie. "Maybe that's why the *oni* is lugging her around with him. Maybe she's like a *key*."

If there wasn't such a sadness always in them about their little lost sister, they might have smiled at the mental picture of the demon warrior sticking Little Harriet in a door lock and turning her like a key. No one smiled now.

"Maybe she *was* his key, you mean," said Knuckleball. "He seems to have lost her now, or she got away, or something."

"And maybe we didn't stay close enough to her. Maybe that's why *we've* lost her now," said Annie.

"Maybe, maybe, maybe," chanted Kiyoshi-chan, smiling.

"Maybe we have to learn a magic spell," said Knuckleball. "Like certain words to open up the garden, Open Sesame or something."

"Maybe there are certain places to stand," said Annie. "Certain times of day. Certain weather conditions. Certain positions, certain gestures. Certain combinations of circumstances. We just have to keep experimenting until we hit on it. The scientific method, and all that."

"Maybe," said Knuckleball, "it's all mathematical somehow. Maybe all the Japanese gardens in the world are arranged in some pattern, and open up according to a regular timetable, like a train schedule."

"Maybe, maybe, maybe," said Kiyoshi-chan again.

"Maybe," said a feathery old voice, "the gardens wish to keep it all . . . a *surprise*."

They turned to see the old *obaa-san* smiling beside them.

"What do you mean, honored person?" asked Annie, very politely, using the full Japanese range of respectful speech for her question.

"You are trying to understand the gardens," said the old woman, "by binding them up in a net of words. If you weave your net well, you think, you can catch the thing you seek."

"Is that wrong?" asked Annie. "We're only trying to understand them so we can use them."

"Wrong?" repeated the old woman, smiling as if the word was a great joke. "Wrong?" She chuckled.

"Help us," said Annie. "We need your help."

"If you catch anything in a net of words," said the old woman, "you have taken the first step to losing it. Words make a great thing small enough to hold in your hand, but what use is it to you then?"

"Could you explain that?" asked Annie.

"The ocean washes the whole world," said the old *obaa-san*, "but if you take your ink brush and write the character for Ocean on a piece of rice paper so you can hold it in your hand, can you sail a boat on that piece of paper?"

"I don't think I understand," said Annie.

"And I *know* I don't," said Knuckleball. "I still think we need the scientific method."

"Good," said the old *obaa-san*, but it wasn't at all clear what she was calling good. "It is time for dinner." She gestured toward the house and shuffled in that direction, bowed almost in half.

As they went back to the house, Knuckleball lagged behind to speak to Annie.

"Annie, I've been thinking," he said. "We're finally in a place where we can call Mom and Dad and let them know where we are. I haven't seen a phone *here,* but there must be one somewhere that we can use."

"I don't think that would work," said Annie. "Trust me."

"Why not?" asked Knuckleball, persistent. "Just because we have no money with us? Can't we just call collect?"

"That's not the problem," said Annie.

"Well, what is?" said Knuckleball. "You're hiding something from me. Does it have something to do with that *Yazu stuff?*"

"*Later*, Knuckler," said Annie, in a no-nonsense voice. They went in to dinner.

CHAPTER 10

From Bad to Worse in the Dead End Mine

Q.J. and Libby wandered back along the impossible tunnel, the hand-hewn mine with no entrances. They felt drawn back to the end with the stone garden, as to a familiar place. They stepped across the tiny stream and paused for a second on its bank.

"Nothing bigger than a tadpole could get in or out this way," said Q.J., pointing to the stream. "It hasn't exactly cut a very big channel through here. Looks like *ghosts* carved out this tunnel."

"Brrrr," said Libby. "I wish you hadn't said that."

In fact, there was no apparent point of entrance for the stream at all. It trickled out of the wall near the ceiling, then washed down the side of the cave in a wide, thin, steady sheet of falling water. Having made its scanty way across the cave floor, it then disappeared into the rocky rubble at the base of the other wall.

"Can we at least drink it?" asked Libby. "I'm very thirsty."

"I would think so," said Q.J. "It looks very clean. Look how it sparkles in my light. But it'll be ice cold, I bet."

Libby got down on her hands and knees and scooped up some of the water to drink. She sat up making a pained expression.

"Ow!" she said. "Feels like my teeth are frozen."

Q.J. was paying no attention. She was playing the beam along all the walls, looking for any kind of opening at all. By shining the light directly back toward the next crook in the cave, she could just see past it the dim shapes of the stone garden, its lantern and "trees."

"Almost home," she said. "It's not really much of a tunnel."

She was surprised at herself for not feeling more panicky about their situation. Neither of them were hungry, there was a source of water, and it was impossible for there *not* to be an exit from this unimaginable cave. Then suddenly her light dimmed for a second, and fear clutched at her before the little bulb brightened again. She realized then that it was nothing but the light that was giving her hope. She took a deep quivering breath and tried to speak in a steady voice to Libby.

"Let's get back to the garden," she said. "These batteries won't last forever."

They took hands again and started to walk on.

But hardly had they done so when Libby stopped without warning, pulling at Q.J.'s hand.

"Did you hear that?" she asked.

"Hear what?" asked Q.J.

"A *noise*," said Libby. "I don't know *what*, you silly."

They listened.

"Nothing," said Q.J. "It was just the echo of our footsteps."

"Maybe," said Libby.

They started to walk again, but then, just as unexpectedly, Libby pulled to a stop again. Q.J. lurched off balance against the cave wall.

"Lib!" she said. "What are you *doing?*"

"I heard it again," said the little girl. "It's a *sound.* It's not water, and it's not *us.*"

Q.J. stood still and listened, but not for very long. That momentary dimming of their only light had frightened her, and made her impatient. She yanked on Libby's hand.

"Come *on,*" she said. "We're wasting batteries. Don't you get the idea?"

But before they could take two more steps they both heard it, a sound that was impossible to identify. There was something nonrandom, purposeful about it, making it more than just a fall of pebbles or a natural shift in the earth. There was something else, something alive, there in the tunnel with them.

Q.J. looked wide-eyed at Libby. "I'm sorry," she breathed.

Trying not to panic, she swung the beam of light all around them, then back again in a quick sweep, to catch anything that might be trying to sneak up on them. Nothing was there. She swung it around again. Still nothing, not even any jumping shadows in the wild beam of the tiny lamp. The cave was empty.

"What is it?" whispered Libby, gripping Q.J.'s hand with both of hers. "What is it?"

Then Q.J. felt it, a ghostly sprinkle of something across the top of her head and shoulders.

"Hey!" she said in a hoarse whisper.

More particles of something fell on her, then a small hard thing like a pebble hit her shoulder.

"Ow!" she said, aloud. "It's caving in! Run!"

Grabbing Libby's hand, she fled toward the garden,

expecting to hear a roar of collapsing earth behind her. Flinging herself to the ground between the lantern and the crane stone, with Libby shielded below her, she covered her head with her hands. She held her breath. Nothing happened. After several long breathless moments she opened her eyes and turned the beam back down the tunnel. There was nothing new to see.

Perplexed, she turned the beam toward the ceiling for the first time since they had come into the cave. Seeing nothing noteworthy near her, she shone it upward and outward along the tunnel, drew in a sharp breath and stared.

"What is it?" asked Libby, pulling her sister's arm more tightly around her.

Q.J. flicked the beam as far along the ceiling as it would go. There was *something* there, a third of the way back down the passage, an ominous black shape clinging to the ceiling. Even as she stared hard at it, it seemed to move. Her breath caught halfway down her throat as she forced herself to look harder at the shape, trying not to remember that they had walked under it several times already, perhaps had stopped and stood directly under it. The sudden thought that whatever it was must have peered down at them with pale eyes or some other horrible apparatus turned her cold and the beam wavered, but she didn't dare turn it off. The thought of not being able to see the thing was far worse than the danger of showing it exactly where they were. She didn't know what to do. In one instant things had gone from hopeless to hideous. She began to walk backward, drawing Libby with her.

"Hey, Quid!" said Libby. Q.J. tried to hush her.

Better not to give the Thing any more reasons to notice them. "Q.J., it's a hole in the ceiling!" cried Libby.

"What!" said Q.J., forcing herself to look again. She flicked the little lamp beam like a long whip, trying to get it to go farther. It certainly could look like a hole in the ceiling, looked at in a certain way. In fact . . .

"Hey!" shouted Q.J. "You're right, Lib! It's our front door!" She laughed and jumped up, pulling Libby to her feet and dragging her back toward the shadow on the ceiling. "The mystery is solved!" she shouted.

"What are you talking about, Q.J.?" asked Libby, hardly able to keep up with her sister. "It's just a hole in the ceiling!"

"Exactly!" said Q.J. "Look!"

The shadow on the ceiling was a great black opening, perhaps four feet wide. They stood under it and looked up. The weakening beam of the light ventured about thirty or forty feet up the smooth sides of a shaft, perhaps just catching the edge of another level of tunnel up above.

"Q.J.!" shouted Libby, now annoyed and frightened at her sister's strange enthusiasm. "*What good does this do us!* We can't fly!"

"No, Lib, I know," said Q.J. "But we *heard* somebody up there, and stuff was falling on us down the shaft. There must be miners working up there who can rescue us! Don't you *get* it? All we have to do is scream for help. Sooner or later someone will hear us."

The little girl *did* get it, and hope came like sunrise to her face. "Hello!" she called at the top of her lungs. "Help!"

"Help!" cried Q.J. "Help! Help!" they both cried

together. The echoes of their shouts ran up and down the passage and swirled around them like laughing voices, rejoicing and dancing like invisible elves. "Help! Help!" they cried with all their might, and the echoes shouted with them, having a wonderful time.

When they finally ran out of breath they stopped and listened, and when the echoes died away, there was a deep and awful silence. They stood absolutely still for a long time, listening.

"Nothing," said Libby. "Nobody."

"It's *OK*," insisted Q.J., hope still strong in her heart. "Maybe their workday is over. We don't really know what time it is. Let's try again, then wait awhile."

"You mean we might have to stay in here for another whole *night?*" asked Libby, her voice trembling again.

Q.J. squeezed her sister. "It's *OK*, Lib," she said again. "It would be worth it, because we *will* be rescued. But let's try again, now."

They shouted and called again until their voices were croaking, like frogs. Q.J. shone the beam of her little reading light up the shaft.

"It's OK," she said to her little sister, for the third time. "They'll come. We just have to be patient."

Then they both heard it, sounds like faraway steps. Joy rose in them again, and they craned their necks to see up the dimly lit shaft.

"There's a light up there," said Q.J. "Do you see it? Shout!"

"Help! Help!" they shouted with every last ounce of their strength.

There *was* a dull red glow far above, bright enough

now so they could see the clear edge of the upper opening of the shaft. They shouted some more, Q.J. flashing her light on and off upward, heedless of batteries now.

"Someone's there!" cried Libby. "Oh, hello! Help us! Rescue us! Don't go away!"

There was at least one dark silhouette against the red light, of someone apparently looking down the shaft.

"It's just us!" cried Libby. "Get us out of here!"

There was something strange about the shape of the silhouette above, as if the head was very large and maned, like a lion's. Q.J. stopped and stared upward, her mouth opened wide. She laid her hand on Libby's arm. Something large and black seemed to break away from the shape above them.

"Look out!" shouted Q.J., flinging Libby aside, where she crashed against the cave wall. But before Q.J. could save herself, a large stone fell from the shaft, struck her a glancing but dreadful blow on the side of her head, and bounced away with a clash and clatter of echoes. She spun to the side, collapsed to one knee and sprawled on the floor. The little lamp flew from her hand, ricocheting a couple of times before going dark for good. The red light above was gone. The cave was as dark as ever. There was no sound, no sound from where Q.J. had been.

Libby cowered in the corner, terrified at the turn things had taken, the swift death of hope.

"Q.J.!" she said, in a hoarse voice.

There was no answer. This was the most awful thing, this silence of her sister.

"Q.J.!" she shouted. "Answer me!" Fear sometimes made Libby angry, as if she thought the Universe was out to get her. Now rage blazed up in her, trying to drown out the fear. "You answer me, Q.J.!"

She was no ordinary six-year-old. It occurred to her suddenly that Q.J. was still lying directly under the shaft opening, unprotected against more missiles from above. She crawled on hands and knees across the floor, feeling with one hand and then the other. It didn't seem as if it could be difficult to find her sister, who must have fallen only a few feet away. But in the darkness she got confused somehow, and actually seemed to crawl in several wrong directions, and maybe even in a circle, before she finally laid a hand on her sister's warm body.

"I have to get you away from here," she said through her teeth, which were beginning to chatter. If she had been older, and had studied first aid, she would have known that she should never move anyone with a head injury. But she was only six, and all she knew was that horrible stones fell from this shaft, and that she had to get Q.J. away from it. She was so confused now in her directions that she had no idea which way she was going, but it didn't seem to matter now. Toward the stream or toward the garden, either way would get away from the dreadful opening in the ceiling.

She jammed the heels of her sneakers into ruts in the ground, planted her sturdy little back against Q.J.'s back, and pushed with all her might.

"Oof!" she grunted, and Q.J. rolled a quarter turn away from her, toward safety, but not without her head bumping on the ground.

"I'm so *stupid*," said Libby, which anyone else could have told her she wasn't. She pulled off her sweatshirt and tried to put it under where Q.J.'s head would roll next. She planted her feet again and pushed, upward and outward with a terrific heave, and felt Q.J. roll away again, up onto her side and down onto her back.

"Yes!" said Libby. Again she shoved her heels into holes in the uneven floor, and rolled Q.J. another half-turn onto her face again. Again she did it, placing the folded sweatshirt, planting her heels, lifting and heaving. Again, and again. She had no idea how many rolls it would take to get her sister to a safe place, so she did it many more times than seemed necessary. Over and over she rolled her sister, away from that awful hole, until it seemed she had never done anything else but plant her heels, lift, and roll, but still she did it again and again. It was to her complete astonishment that Q.J.'s limp body suddenly rolled up against an obstacle that Libby discovered with her hands was the crane stone.

"Wow!" she said. "We've come a long ways, Q."

For some obscure reason, she still was not satisfied till she had rolled, pushed, and pulled Q.J. into a position between the lantern and the little ridge of trees. She flopped down and laid her head on Q.J.'s warm stomach, exhausted. She felt a deep, weary satisfaction in what she had accomplished, and the fear and anger were almost buried away inside her, or had been burned off in the great effort.

"We've done a good job, Q.J.," she said, and fell fast asleep.

When she awoke, the cave was filled with red light. She sat up with a start and looked around her, but could see nothing strange but the light. It seemed to be coming from the other side of the first bend in the tunnel, perhaps from the ceiling shaft itself. She could see the opening, and it seemed less black than before, as if there were a source of light inside or above it. Then she saw the great rope.

Swaying like a strangely deformed snake, the thickly knotted rope was hanging down from the shaft, and even as she watched, a pair of massive armored legs came swinging down it, followed by the rest of a horrible figure.

"*Oni*," she said to herself, a hopeless fear surging up inside her. "The demon warrior." She sat as still as it was possible for a human being to sit, trying to will herself to be invisible, trying to silence the hammering of her heart in her chest, trying to stop all the breathing and beating and pulsing that her terrified little body insisted on doing.

She noticed in a sort of detached way that the armor of this *oni* was not red and blue, like that of the one who had stolen Little Harriet away, but was black and gold and green. He crouched down in the passageway on his haunches, too tall to stand upright. Red light seemed to pour out of his helmet and through the stitches and chinks of his armor. He said something in a voice like crumbling stone.

Libby froze. There was a burst of harsh laughter, and answering voices, and Libby realized that there were other huge warrior goblins, around the bend, out of sight. There was no hope at all, no hope, only a black wall behind her and cruel demons before her, but she felt from nowhere a strange thrill, almost painful, like happiness. She had no idea why. She felt the warmth of Q.J. through her back and drew strength from the company of her sister.

One of the invisible demon warriors came into sight,

at the bend in the tunnel. He was stooped over almost double, but the ghastly mask of his helmet was looking directly at her. Libby looked back, as if hypnotized.

Later she wondered how long she had been smelling the sweet familiar evergreen breeze before it finally sank in what it was. Years later she still believed that the breeze had been in her nostrils for some time, and that it was this heartbreaking, piercing, lovely breath that had been giving her that strange and joyful hopefulness even in a cave filled with demon warriors. Now, though, she suddenly realized what it meant.

The garden gateway was open again. The stone garden, which had dumped them here in this black cave, was now beckoning them somewhere else, any-where else, away from danger.

Staring back at the huge demon, she slowly moved her feet until they were propped against the crane stone of the garden. It was better leverage than she had ever had yet for the rolling of Q.J. The piney breeze was pouring over her shoulder, from beyond the little ridge of trees. All she had to do was get Q.J. over that ridge.

She stared back hard at the demon warrior, who was still peering into the gloom of the garden end of the tunnel. She wondered if he also could sense that there was an open garden gateway here. She wondered if he could even see her. For some unknown reason, as a sort of reckless experiment, she stuck her tongue out at him. He didn't respond.

Wedging her sturdy bottom as far under Q.J. as it would go, Libby gathered up her strength for the great-est and most important effort of her little life. "Oof!" she cried out as she heaved upward and backward. The demon warriors roared, hearing her. Q.J. rolled over once, to the top of the ridge, where the stone trees stopped her from going over.

"Oh, please!" gasped Libby, leaping up and over the ridge herself. She grabbed Q.J.'s arm and tried to *pull* her over, which is the hardest thing to do with a heavy weight. Two, three, four, five, six goblin warriors came stooping around the bend, swords drawn. They still seemed to be having trouble seeing into the garden, but suddenly with another gravelly roar they leaped forward.

"Oh, please!" wailed Libby, pulling on Q.J.'s arm with all her might. And even as she pulled, she felt the stone floor dissolving below her as the tiny garden enlarged and rushed outward expanding, to take her into itself and far away.

CHAPTER 11

Annie and Knuckleball Almost Miss Kyoto

It was on a lovely, dream-like Sunday in April when Kiyoshi-chan's father took his son and the two American children on an excursion to Kyoto.

"It is the ancient capital of Japan," he said. "You *must* see it before you go back to Massachusetts."

"And," said Kiyoshi-chan with a significant look at Annie and Knuckleball, "it has many, many temple gardens."

"Yes, yes, yes," said his father, raising an eyebrow. "I know that you must see your *gardens*. I will close my market tomorrow so we can spend two days there. Sunday night we will spend with my sister in Uji."

Annie and Knuckleball had finally given their whole story to Kiyoshi-chan's family, and though the father had laughed at the parts he couldn't believe in, the mother and old grandparents had taken it all very seriously.

"We will show you gardens then," the father had finally said. "Until your parents come to get you. We will show you gardens and gardens and gardens until you decide to go home by airplane instead. Of course traveling by gardens is cheaper, but at least airplanes take off on a schedule." He laughed, not unkindly, but as if he thought of them as two rather nice lunatics.

"*Domo arigato gozaimashita*," Annie and Knuckleball had both said. "You are being very kind to us."

So they traveled to Kyoto by train, leaving by the first departures on Sunday morning. The children slept for the first part, laying their heads on each other's shoulders as the train rocked and rattled along, and as the aisles in front of them grew gradually more crowded with curious people. There were many stops, the next station often visible from the last, and the noise of hissing brakes, scuffling feet, and tinny announcements all mingled with the children's dreams and drowsy thoughts.

They changed trains several times, once at a great booming, roaring madhouse of a station where they had to run up flights of steps, weaving through the crowd, and then down onto another platform, where they were jammed at the last second into a packed train by uniformed attendants.

"I'm glad we don't have to do this very often," said Knuckleball, peering up at Annie from his place in the crush of bodies. "I can hardly breathe."

"I would think there would be a *Shinkansen* line to Kyoto from Tokyo," said Annie to Kiyoshi-chan's father. "The bullet train. Wouldn't that be faster, and less crowded?"

He looked at her in a bewildered way, so she wondered if she had offended him. Maybe the famous bullet train was too expensive, and she had hurt his feelings by mentioning it? But then with a sick feeling she remembered the whole business about *Yazu* and Taiho and the rest, and she wondered weakly when the

Shinkansen had first been built. She turned and looked out the window, trying to put it from her mind.

As they left Tokyo behind the crush eased somewhat, and after another change or two they were able to get seats again, but on opposite sides of the train, and separated. Annie gazed out the far window, watching the tiled roofs, neat green fields, and dusty roads flowing by. There were bicycles everywhere, and men and women walking here and there with huge loads on their backs. In places there were children playing, but once there was a schoolyard full of uniformed children doing some kind of organized Sunday activity. The windows were open, so at each stop a rich complexity of smells poured in on the spring breeze, scents of sweet flower blossoms, wood smoke, and hot railroad tar, grease, and metal. There was something poignant in this unfamiliar blend of familiar odors, and Annie found herself excited by it, without knowing why.

Kiyoshi-chan's father read his newspaper for hours, dozing occasionally while sitting straight up. Annie glanced over at his paper and tried to imagine someone being able to read such a complicated language so easily. She knew a few of the difficult *kanji* characters, and more of the simpler phonetic symbols, but it boggled her mind that anyone could read everyday news, sports articles, or the goofy-looking comics in such a complicated form of writing. It seemed like the sort of writing made only for poetry or mystical thoughts. Or maybe incantations for opening philosophical gardens, she said to herself. After trying to puzzle out a bit of it, she shook her head and looked back out the window.

They arrived at Kyoto Station after a train journey of over five hours, and stumbled out onto the sidewalk, stiff and ready to see sights.

"First we eat lunch," said Kiyoshi-chan's father, and untying a large silk wrapper, he passed around a *bento* to each one. Each *bento* was a box divided into compartments, filled with helpings of rice, vegetables, pickles, and small slices of fruit. They sat on the concrete ledge outside the station and ate. The sun was warm on their heads.

"So how many temples are there in Kyoto?" asked Knuckleball, picking up a piece of fried pork with his chopsticks.

Kiyoshi-chan's father said something, with his mouth full. Annie stared at him.

"Excuse me?" she said. "How many did you say?"

He swallowed. "Two thousand," he said, and smiled. He stuffed in another heaped mouthful of rice.

"Two thousand!" she said. "Two thousand?"

"*Hai*," he nodded, chewing. "Yes. Two thousand."

Annie bit into a pickled radish and chewed several times. "And how many of these have gardens?" she asked.

"All of them, of course," he said. "What is a temple without a garden?"

"And are there other gardens in Kyoto," asked Knuckleball. "Besides the temple ones?"

"Of course," said Kiyoshi-chan's father. "What is a home without a garden?"

"How can we possibly see them all?" wailed Annie.

"You can't, of course," he said. "But it only takes one to *whisk* you back to Boston, like a magic carpet."

He chuckled, cleaning out the last grains of rice from his lunch and popping them in his mouth one by one with his chopsticks. "But regardless," he said, "if you want to see philosophical gardens, Kyoto is the place to come."

Annie and Knuckleball looked at each other.

"Then what are we waiting for?" said Annie. So it was that the Kyoto trip became a disaster. Like the worst sort of tourist they bolted from one place to another all afternoon, in fact until the evening became too dark to see a thing. Then they took a local train to Uji and stayed the night in the tiny home of Kiyoshi-chan's aunt, and were back in Kyoto before seven o'clock the next morning, zigzagging from one garden to another through all the length and breadth of the old city.

Annie would regret this for years afterward, until she finally was able to return to the incredible city of Kyoto again, and to see it the way it was meant to be seen. They fled from temple to temple, garden to garden, shrine to shrine, hardly seeing the breathtaking clouds of cherry blossoms in full flower around them, never taking a moment to soak in the peacefulness of a dry, bright, sun-washed Zen garden. Years later Annie would still remember and regret the grim look that gradually settled on the face of Kiyoshi-chan's father and of Kiyoshi-chan himself, realizing that she and Knuckleball must have seemed those days like the very crassest kind of American sightseer. Though only the proprietor of a little country market, Kiyoshi-chan's father, like all Japanese, loved the beauty and metaphysics of nature, and was a minor poet in his own village. Not believing in their desperate need to find a garden gateway, he could only interpret their headlong rush through Kyoto as the greatest possible insensitivity to beauty, to delicacy, to sun and bloom and wind and tree.

But Annie and Knuckleball could only think of lost Little Harriet, and they galloped from one place to another, towing their Japanese friends behind them. They looked everywhere for likely places, sniffing their way through the heavy scent of spring flowers for a familiar cool, piney breeze, stepping into bright shrubbery and behind stone pagodas and under twisted little evergreens, hoping against hope to feel the earth dissolve beneath their feet and to find themselves swept away on the trail of Little Harriet again. But the ground was always solid, and every hint of an evergreen smell turned out to be the smell of an actual pine or larch or cedar, almost lost in the overwhelming Kyoto riot of April flowers.

They saw the Kinkakuji, or Golden Pavilion, and the Ginkakuji, or Silver Pavilion, both magnificent in their settings of ponds and trees. At the insistence of Kiyoshichan's father they took a moment to dip water and drink with a long-handled tin cup from the famous spring of the Clear Water Temple, Kiyomizudera. They saw the many-roofed pagoda of Daigoji, and the kilometers of red *torii* at the Shinto shrine of Fushimiinari.

They saw the famous dry rock garden of Ryoanji, and at the Tendai temple of Sanzenin they saw but hardly noticed the lovely moss-mounded garden, with its shrubs sculpted into fat little heaps, like clusters of very docile green farm animals.

After all this, Annie finally paused in one place. She never knew the name of it, but it was a deep bamboo grove, with the stalks of bamboo growing almost too tightly to walk between. The pointed leaves overhead were entangled together into a green roof, through which the Monday afternoon sun could barely filter. She looked into the grove and was caught, as if by a mystic power.

"Come on, Knuckler," she whispered.

"Yes!" breathed Knuckleball, seeing into the grove himself. "This is just the kind of place."

They stepped into the grove, while Kiyoshi-chan and his father looked after them, puzzled. It was like stepping into an underwater world, the kind that comes to life in so many Japanese fairy tales of the realm of the Dragon King. Liquid green light flowed around them, the ground was soft underfoot, and the bamboo spoke in a hushed whisper, like the sound of gentle rain. They took each other's hands wordlessly. There was a breeze through the grove, not the piney mountain breeze they were looking for, but maybe related to it, somehow.

Annie turned back toward their friends, whom they could barely see through the gently swaying stalks. "We have really not done well," she said. "We have to go talk to them."

"OK," said Knuckleball, understanding.

They emerged into the bright sunlight, where the man and the boy waited for them, wearing expressions of long but weary patience. The two American children bowed very low to them both, one at a time.

"We have been very rude," Annie said. "We have been a little out of our minds. Please forgive us. We have hurt you, and we are sorry."

Kiyoshi-chan grinned, and his father bowed to Annie, insisting that no such apology was necessary. When he straightened, his face was eased of its frown.

"Show us what *you* would like us to see," said Annie, "in the time we have left."

So they went to just one more place, another nameless temple with a garden. There they sat as the shadows lengthened, watching three turtles on a rock, listening to the *thock . . . thock . . . thock* of a bamboo water pipe, which filled from a falling trickle and tipped, pouring its water into a stone basin. No garden gateway showed itself, but a great peace flowed around them, and Annie and Knuckleball both felt some of their distress fall away.

"Everything will be OK," said Annie. "We'll find her yet."

They left Kyoto just before dusk, and slept most of the way back to Kashiwa, despite all the jostle and jolts of the trains. When they got back to Kiyoshi-chan's little house it was like coming home, and in a short time his mother had a simple but steaming meal on the table, with bowls of tofu soup and heaped white rice.

Kiyoshi-chan's *obaa-san* knelt beside Annie, her hands folded in her lap. "You must not have found it," she said, "or you would not still be here."

"I was still trying to catch it in my net," said Annie. "I'm afraid that even if it was there I would have missed it. I was like a crazy woman."

The old grandmother chuckled. "You seem to be sane again," she said. "Maybe you are ready to find it now."

"Maybe," said Annie.

The *obaa-san* looked at Kiyoshi-chan's father. "There is one more place you must take them," she said.

He rolled his eyes. "Where is that?"

"To the shrine of Sumiyoshi-no-Kami," said the old woman.

"The god of poetry?" said the man.

"And to its garden," said the *obaa-san*. "The Garden of a Thousand Worlds."

"But that is six hours from here, in the mountains," said Kiyoshi-chan's father, with obvious reluctance. "I would have to borrow Sakamoto-san's car. And it is only one garden. Such a trip for one garden."

"Yes," said the old woman.

Annie and Knuckleball looked at each other.

"Here we go again," said Knuckleball.

"Let's do this one right," said Annie.

CHAPTER 12

The Knock on the Gate

The top of the moss mound *was* moving; there was no doubt about it. There seemed to be a lump growing there, and chunks of moss and dirt were falling away.

'Siah was shaking like a leaf. "It's something else scary, isn't it?" he said. He stopped suddenly, and got a wrathful look on his face. "Well, I'm *sick* of scary things!" he shouted, and grabbing the old priest's cane he squeezed through the hedge of trees and started clambering to the top of the mound. "I'm gonna *whack* that thing before it even gets out of the ground." In no time he was thumping away at the heaving lump with the sturdy staff.

"'Siah!" yelled Owen Greatheart, trying to squeeze through after his brother, but getting stuck halfway. Basho the monkey scrambled through easily and swung up the little hill after 'Siah. "Get back here!" cried Owen Greatheart. "You have no idea—"

But before he could finish, there was another cry, a shriek of anger and indignation. "*'Siah!*" yelled a voice. "You stop hitting me! You wait till I tell *Mom!*"

"Libby!" shouted Owen Greatheart in astonishment. "It's *Libby*, 'Siah! Stop it!"

But the little boy had already stopped thumping with his stick and was hauling away on his sister with all his might. "It's Libby!" he was shouting with delight.

"Owen, come help me get her out of here. She's *stuck*."

"I'm *not* stuck," argued Libby. She and 'Siah could rarely speak without arguing, no matter what country they were in. "It's *Q.J.* I can't get her through."

By this time Owen Greatheart and the old priest had dashed around the end of the hedge and were on top of the mound themselves, pulling on Q.J.'s arm, which was the only visible part of her. Libby was out completely, and pulling fiercely with the others.

"Careful," said Owen Greatheart. "We'll pull her arm right out of the socket if we don't watch it."

"No!" gritted Libby through her teeth. "We *have* to pull. They've got her by the *feet*."

"*Who's* got her?" asked Owen Greatheart, but wasted no time trying to dig away the top of the soft mound with his fingers. Q.J.'s head popped through, her eyes bulging wide open. She was fully conscious now, though the side of her head was an ugly mass of blood.

"Something's pulling on my legs!" she wailed. "Pull me!"

She got another arm through, and waiting hands grabbed it.

"It's those big goblins," said Libby, planting her feet and straining backward. "There's a whole army of them down there."

"Kick your legs!" shouted 'Siah. "Kick 'em right in the nose!"

"I'm trying!" sobbed Q.J. "There are too many of them!"

There was no doubt about it, she was beginning to slip backward into the mound. They were losing.

"No!" shouted Owen Greatheart. "We can't let her go!"

He turned to the old priest, who seemed to be uselessly poking his stick into the top of the mound on all sides of Q.J., as if trying to find a soft spot.

"Help us!" screamed Owen Greatheart. "We need you to pull! Or does *that* go against your philosophy?" He was almost beside himself with rage.

The old priest smiled gently at him. "No," he said. "It doesn't. But this fits it better." He hugged his stout staff to himself, having retrieved it from 'Siah. "*Sayonara*," he said. He jumped lightly into the air, the skirts of his robe billowing out around him. There was still a small smile on his face as he plunged downward, disappearing into the mound as if it were water.

Seconds later, Q.J. came flying out of the ground as if she had been thrown, and tumbled down to the bottom of the mound. A great hand, armored in black and purple, thrust upward out of the mound, then was snatched back.

Everyone rushed down to gather around Q.J. She blinked and tried to shake the dirt out of her hair. "Ow!" she said, and held her head.

"You're hurt bad," said Owen Greatheart. "We need to get some help for you."

"I feel OK," said Q.J. "But this hurts some."

'Siah looked back upward. "Is he coming back?" he asked. "I hope he's coming *back*."

But the top of the mound was quiet now, looking all chewed and trampled. Nothing moved there at all.

"He doesn't have a chance against an army of demon warriors," said Owen Greatheart. "What'll he do, wave his old stick vigorously around *their* bodies?"

"He didn't *seem* worried," said Libby. "He must have had a plan of some kind."

No one knew what to do or say. There was a solemn pause that felt like a memorial hush for the old priest.

"Look, Q," said Owen Greatheart finally. "There's water down the path. Let's at least try to wash the dirt off the wound."

For the first time they turned and looked down at what they could see of the Garden of a Thousand Worlds. It was obviously designed to be seen only a little bit at a time, with mossy mounds and boulders and hedges and clusters of trees arranged to divide one view from another. It was undeniably beautiful, a little wilder and more overgrown than other Japanese gardens they had seen, but nothing extraordinary. They could see over it to some taller trees that seemed to be its far boundary.

"It's not very big," said Owen Greatheart. "Pretty small, in fact. Doesn't look like a thousand worlds could fit in here."

"It seems very old, though," said Q.J., leaning on one elbow. "Look at the moss everywhere, even on the trees. And some of those trees are ancient. What is this place?"

They filled her in quickly, with whatever information they knew from Basho.

"And it's *supposed* to be seven hundred years old," said Owen Greatheart. "If it didn't look a little old we'd feel cheated, I suppose. Let's go."

Basho the monkey flipped a couple of times and came out right side up, facing them. "Silly people," he said. "Weren't we warned about going into this Garden?

Didn't he say we would never come out again?"

Owen Greatheart hesitated. "I don't think he really *knew*," he said. "I still think maybe he was just giving us the old Chamber of Commerce line. You know, exaggerating the uniqueness of the local tourist attractions."

"You forget," said Basho. "They don't *invite* tourists here. Tourists are actively discouraged from visiting. There's a Keep Out sign on the gate."

"True," said Owen Greatheart, scratching his head. "But we need to get in there *somehow*. It's a gateway of some kind for sure, and we need it to get to Little Harriet."

"In a hall of a thousand doors, in which you only get to try *one*," said Basho, "how would you decide which one leads to Little Harriet?"

"I don't know," said Owen Greatheart. "I don't know."

There was a knock on the garden gate. They looked at each other, startled.

"Who could that be?" asked Q.J.

They all shrugged, perplexed about what to do.

"How do we know?" asked 'Siah. "We don't live here."

"It doesn't seem," said Basho, "like the kind of gate one would knock on."

"Especially with a Keep Out sign on it," said Libby.

"Unless," said Owen Greatheart, "it's someone who can't read the sign."

"Or someone who *can* read it," said Basho, "but really has to get in for some reason."

"And is too courteous just to barge in without knocking," said Owen Greatheart.

"Like *we* did," said Basho.

There was another knock.

"It certainly couldn't be one of those *demons*," said Libby. "They don't seem like the type of people who *ever* knock."

"True," said Owen Greatheart.

"It must be Annie," said 'Siah, who was back on Owen's shoulders, one of his favorite places.

They all looked at him in surprise.

"Why do you say *that?*" asked Q.J. "O little detective."

"Because," said 'Siah. "Just think about it. Annie can't read much Japanese. She really has to get in for some reason. *And* she's the politest person I know. She would never go into a place without being *invited*."

"Pretty smart, little brother," said Owen Greatheart. "But I don't know if I'm ready to go open that gate yet."

"Besides," laughed 'Siah, "I can *see* her. Hi, Annie!" he shouted at the top of his lungs, waving wildly and trying to stand up on Owen Greatheart's shoulders.

"You little *twerp!*" shouted Owen Greatheart, and they all tumbled shouting down the hill and around the hedge, flinging open the gate. There was Annie standing there grinning, and there was Knuckleball running up the flagstones toward them, and there was what looked like a whole Japanese family of all ages following behind, smiling and waving.

"Hi, guys," said Annie. "Here we all are."

CHAPTER 13

One Way Home

Demon warriors and dead-end mines, Kyoto shrines and cherry blossoms, strange old priests and snow monkeys. There was so much catching up to do, and everyone tried to do it all at once. They sat in the moss outside the garden gate, and Kiyoshi-chan and his family watched in a bemused way as the American children chattered in a wild combination of English and Japanese, trying to find out where everyone had been, and what had happened in each place. In between all the news, there was general concern about Q.J.'s injury, and about the need to find some clean water and bandages.

"In the Garden," said Owen Greatheart. "There's plenty of water there. We have to go in sooner or later anyway."

"And we can rip up our sleeves for bandages," said Libby. "That's what they do in books. Each person can donate one sleeve."

"Oh, that should be enough," said Q.J., pulling her little sister's braid. "With twelve sleeves you could wrap me up like a mummy."

Meanwhile, Kiyoshi-chan's mother was untying a huge silk-wrapped bundle that her husband had packed in on his back. "Is *sunakku*," she said. "For eating."

"A *snack?*" said Knuckleball. "Looks more like a banquet, from the size of it."

And so it proved to be. By the time she had spread it out on the moss, everyone realized how hungry they had become, and how glad they were that she had brought no less. It took astonishingly little time for the *sunakku* of *inari-zushi* and a variety of side dishes to disappear. The children thanked her over and over, while stuffing their mouths with a "dessert" of salty *osenbei* crackers.

"We need to take some bags of these home with us," said Owen Greatheart. "If we end up taking a plane home, our luggage allowance should give us room for a ton of *sunakku*. We've got no other baggage to take up space."

"A plane?" said Knuckleball. "Does that mean we're not just taking the garden gateways back?"

"*Just?*" laughed Owen Greatheart. "You make it sound so simple."

"There's no way we should even *try* it," said logical Q.J. "Now we know of *two* times that a garden gateway has re-opened to work in reverse, but at least in one of those cases we ended up in a whole new place, not the original point. How could we possibly find our way back to Boston? Squib and I went from the azalea garden to the mine, but then we ended up *here*."

"And what was the other time?" asked Libby, puzzled.

"Little Harriet," said Q.J. "Escaping from big bad Kiyoshi-chan in the middle of the night. She went right back into the garden she came out of, but who knows where she was before that or where she went from there?"

"Unpredictable," said Annie. "That's the key word with the gardens. Surprise. I don't think they have a scientific explanation in the usual sense of the word." She glanced at Kiyoshi-chan's *obaa-san*, who was still munching toothlessly on something, apparently oblivious to the conversation.

"Of course not," said Owen Greatheart. "It's obviously some kind of magic."

"I suppose," said Annie. "But think about it. In our culture, *magic* is not really a whole lot different than science. In all our old stories, magic is mechanical. It goes by formulas just like science or technology. If you say Open Sesame, the cave has no choice but to open. Find the right formula in the book of spells, say it on tiptoes with your eyes crossed, and presto! the evil witch turns into a toad, or whatever. It's just like moving the mouse or tapping keys on our computer keyboard. If this is magic, it's not like *our* kind of magic at all."

"So?" said Knuckleball. "Is there a point to this lecture, Annie Granny?"

"*So*," said Q.J., flicking a little larch cone off Knuckleball's left cheek, "she's just saying that, if we have a *known* destination, in the real world, we're better off with a nice slow boat."

Annie said nothing.

"But what about finding Little Harriet?" said Owen Greatheart, raising an eyebrow. "No boat or airplane can help us there."

"True," said Annie. "That's a different story."

"We have no choice," said Q.J. "We *have* to use the garden gateways to find her. Something has been directing us so far, whether it's been the demons themselves, the gardens, or something totally different, and whatever it is seems to want to keep us on the trail of Little Harriet. There's probably no good explanation for that little explosion that separated us last time. I think the demons have a tendency to derange whatever they're using, even if it's this whole garden thing. I guess that *this* Garden will take us to Little Harriet, whatever the old priest said."

"I think that might be what *he* thought, too," said Owen Greatheart. "He didn't really say not. He just sort of said we might regret wherever we ended up, and not be able to get back."

"That's a chance we have to take," said Q.J. "Then at least we'll all be lost together, instead of Little Harriet being lost all by herself."

"I disagree," said Owen Greatheart. "Listen, I have an idea. Doesn't it make sense for only one or two of us to try the Garden? Like maybe Annie and me?"

"And what's the point of *that?*" asked Knuckleball. "I agree with Q.J. that it's bad for us to split up. We *have* to stick together."

"But listen," said Owen Greatheart. "Suppose two of us go, and whether or not we ever find Little Harriet, we can't get back? Then at least four of us are still here in the real world, and can hop a plane back to the States. Better only three of us lost forever, wandering some strange weird world, than *all* of us. Think of Dad, and Mom."

This provoked an uncomfortable silence. No one could deny the sense of it.

"And," said Owen Greatheart, "probably the two of us would have as much chance of rescuing Little Harriet from wherever she is, as all six of us together. I mean, the little kids might just get in the way."

"Hey!" yelled Libby.

"I can knock you over any time, you big Owen,"

said 'Siah, jumping on the head of his biggest brother. "In fact, I don't think you can rescue Little Harriet *without* me and Squibby."

"You *are* a scary pair," said Owen Greatheart, wrestling 'Siah in the moss. "I can't deny that. Ow!" He sat back suddenly against the garden fence, testing with his fingers for loose teeth. In the tussle 'Siah's hard head had clunked him in the mouth. "We could just use your head for a battering ram," he mumbled. "I think this tooth is loose, you little tiger."

"I have to agree with Owen," said Q.J. suddenly. "It's logical."

"Me too," said Knuckleball. "But I have to be one of the ones to go."

"Me too," said 'Siah and Libby in unison.

"No way," said Owen Greatheart. "The two oldest ones go, and the rest of you wait here. If we don't come back, then call Mom and Dad and take a plane home. Who knows? Finish that Japanese garden in the living room and one day the three of us may come strolling out of it."

"Cool," said Knuckleball, intrigued by the idea. "But I'm coming."

"No, you're not," said Owen Greatheart. "You stay here with your buddy Kiyoshi-chan."

"Try and make me," said Knuckleball. "How could you *possibly* rescue Little Harriet without my expertise?"

"Expertise in *what?*" said Owen Greatheart. "We don't have a clue what we'll find when we get there."

"Bear in mind," said Knuckleball gravely, "that I am the only known human being *ever* to have knocked the head off a demon warrior and lived to tell the tale. How can you ignore that?"

"Except for Momotaro the Peach Boy," said Kiyoshi-chan.

"Excuse me?" said Knuckleball.

"We have a very old story in Japan," said Kiyoshi-chan, "about a little boy named Momotaro, who slaughtered a whole castleful of demons. Except he didn't have a fence post. He only had a pheasant, a dog, and a monkey."

"Ha!" said Basho the monkey. "You mean the *monkey* only had a pheasant, a dog, and a *boy*."

"There's no comparison," said Knuckleball. "See? This peach kid had reinforcements. But where does the peach part come in?"

"Forget it, Knuckles. Let's get on with this," said Q.J. "We've got to make a decision, *now*. Little Harriet's not getting any less lost while we sit here squabbling. What's with you, Annie? You haven't said a word in at least three minutes."

Annie certainly did seem to have something else on her mind.

"Yeah, what's up, Gran?" said Knuckleball. "You've been covering something up from way back."

Annie sighed, with deep reluctance. "All right," she said. "I've got some things to explain to everyone. We can't really go on without it."

"Well, let's get it over with," said Q.J.

"The problem," said Annie, "has to do with getting home again."

"Money, you mean?" said Owen Greatheart. "If we call Dad can't he get it to us somehow? I mean, I know it's expensive and he's not made of money, but I *think* he'd want as many of us back as possible."

"Not money," said Annie. "It has to do with a conversation I overheard between Knuckleball and Kiyoshi-chan. You need to hear this, Owen. Kiyoshi-chan, try telling us again. Who were those Red Sox players you were talking to Knuckleball about? Remember?"

"Of course I remember," said Kiyoshi-chan. He felt a flush of indignation and betrayal again, looking sidelong at his friend Knuckleball. The small hurt of that afternoon had never quite gone away, though he had convinced himself that perhaps American children treated even their best friends this way. "*Yazu*, you mean?" he said. "And *Tonee-See? And Ree-ko? And Jimu Ro-nu-bu-ru-gu?*"

"Right," said Annie. "Owen, do you know those names?"

"Of course," said Owen Greatheart. "*Yazu* must be Yaz. Carl Yastrzemski, that is. And then obviously Tony Conigliaro and Rico Petrocelli. What was the other one again?" Kiyoshi-chan repeated it. "Naturally," said Owen Greatheart. "Jim Lonborg, twenty-two wins that season. How do you know so much about the '67 Red Sox, Kiyoshi-chan? My *dad* was a kid then. A little before your time."

Kiyoshi-chan looked completely flummoxed. None of this made any sense at all. It made him wonder again whether the American children had learned some strange dialect of Japanese that they switched into occasionally, by accident.

"No," said Annie quietly. "They're not before his time at all."

All the siblings looked at their oldest sister.

Owen Greatheart scratched his head. "OK," he

said. "I give up. Explain, Annie."

"It's no riddle," said Annie. "It's just that the gardens do more than transport us across space."

Owen Greatheart squinted at her, with a somewhat sick expression.

"No," he said.

"Yes," said Annie.

"Do you mean *time*, Granny?" said Knuckleball excitedly. "*Cool!*"

"Not so cool," said Annie. "We're in *1968*, Knuckles."

"So?" said Knuckleball. "That's what's so cool."

"*Think*, O brainless one," said Annie. "The *coolness* of it disappears when you realize what it means. How can any of us take a plane back to Boston? Mom and Dad won't even be there for years yet! We're lost in *time*, Peach Boy, with no way home."

Knuckleball, 'Siah, and Libby took this in with wide eyes, suddenly realizing the implications. The thought of that friendly airplane that seemed all ready to take them home whenever they really wanted it, had for a long time been an unspoken comfort to them all. Their faces began to crumble into despair. Annie got down on her knees quickly and wrapped them in her long arms.

"But there's still hope," she said. "It's only airplanes and trains and boats that can't take us across time. Do you know what that means?"

The little children shook their heads, slowly.

"It means we're *all* doing the Garden," said Annie brightly. "Together."

CHAPTER 14

The Garden of
a Thousand Worlds

The Garden opened to receive the six American children and Basho the monkey, who had insisted on coming along. They said good-bye to their Japanese friends, thanking them for all of their help. But as Kiyoshi-chan and Knuckleball bowed their sad farewells to each other, there seemed to be a lively consultation still going on among the adults of the family. In fact, the old *obaa-san* seemed actually to be *arguing*, showing more animation than the American children had ever seen in her. When the children made it clear that they were going at last into the Garden, Kiyoshi-chan's parents were polite but distracted in their good-byes, as if something was still unsettled.

This distant sort of farewell was disappointing, but before they had even gotten beyond the mossy mound that had been their deepest penetration into the Garden earlier, the gate banged behind them and Kiyoshi-chan came bursting through.

"Kiyoshi-chan!" cried Knuckleball. "What are you doing in here?"

"I'm coming with you," said Kiyoshi-chan, flushed with excitement.

"How did *that* happen?"

"My *grandmother* said I had to," said Kiyoshi-chan, incredulously. "That I might be *needed*. My mother said No. My father said that it's only another garden, and that we would all be coming out again almost as quickly as we went in, so why not? My mother said that it's *not* only a garden. My grandmother said that she was right and my father was wrong, it's not only a garden, but that I would be all right. My grandfather didn't say anything. I think all four of them thought each other was crazy. Finally they just said Go. So here I am!"

This all came out in a breathless rush, so that when Kiyoshi-chan finished he had to stop and recover. Knuckleball laughed. "It can't get any better than this!" he said, clapping Kiyoshi-chan on the back.

"Except for finding Little Harriet," said Q.J. "*That* would be better."

"I know that, Quid," said Knuckleball, annoyed that she would have thought he might have forgotten it.

"No fighting," said Annie. "Let's go."

They went around the bend at last, the one they had been able to see from their first entrance into the Garden. The path was made of smooth dark river rocks, so glossy that it seemed they should have been slippery but weren't. Dark green moss grew between the flat stones, which were spaced at irregular but comfortable intervals along the path. The children were hushed as they came out of the little curve and found themselves in a long straightaway, thickly hedged on both sides and overhung with maples.

"Hm," said Owen Greatheart. "I wouldn't have thought this was here, from what I saw up on the mound.

I would have expected more of a twisty sort of path right here. But I guess I couldn't really see it too clearly."

There was nothing to say to this. They walked slowly down the pathway, stepping from one smooth dark stone to the next. There were birds in the trees overhead, but because of the thickness of the foliage they were invisible. The Garden seemed a sleepy, trance-like place, for the moment.

"Doesn't it feel like we're going downhill?" asked Q.J. "But the path looks perfectly level."

It was true. Something gave the distinct impression that they were descending deeper into a valley, but their eyes told them clearly otherwise.

"Odd," said Owen Greatheart.

The green shadowiness of the pathway deepened as they went along it, the foliage overhead thickening and the bordering hedges drawing in, narrowing. The end of the straightaway was in sight, but was in such deep shadow that it wasn't until they had almost reached it that they realized it was a thick stand of black bamboo, dripping with rain. The path of glossy stepping-stones meandered sharply to the left through the bamboo, just wide enough for single file. They entered the grove with Basho in the lead.

"That rain came on us in a hurry," said Annie, squinting up at the overcast sky. "I sure thought it was a clear enough day outside the Garden."

"It's just a drizzle," said Owen Greatheart, but it was enough of a drizzle for the spear-shaped bamboo leaves above to trickle steadily onto their heads until they were soaked. The overcast grove was in deep emerald shade, its ground covered with tall streaming ferns. The ferns themselves seemed to glow with a soft green light of their own against the black stems of the bamboo.

"This just might be the most beautiful place I have ever seen," said Q.J.

"Yes," said Owen Greatheart.

They finally came out of the bamboo into mottled sunlight, and onto an earthen trail that wound steeply upward.

"Well!" said Annie. "Fickle weather."

The trail plunged ahead into a great crowd of boulders, some of them towering twenty feet into the air. The path itself, making its way between the boulders, became a rough stone staircase that looked from below like a rushing torrent, a river frozen into weathered stone.

"Up we go," said Knuckleball. "Looks like we're in for a mountain climb."

"Looks like it," said Q.J.

But despite its steepness, the natural steps of the rocky staircase were at easy intervals, and they went up it quickly, toward a thick stand of wild pines. There was an evergreen wind all around them as they came to the top of the stone staircase and found themselves overlooking still another, entirely new landscape.

"This *can't* all fit in here," said Owen Greatheart.

This, once again, had no answer. In front of them was a steep bank, down which they could look on the top of a stone lantern and a small pagoda, almost as if they were on a mountaintop looking down on human habitations of the world. The path bent quickly off to the right, making its way down a dwindling ridge until it let them off on the smooth stone shore of a large pond. They could see all around the pond, which as Owen Greatheart pointed out, should not all by itself have fit into the actual acreage of the Garden. At their feet was a beach of smooth round stones, but to their left the pond was edged by massive rock formations sprinkled with maple leaves. The air here was cool, almost October-like.

"Why a bridge to nowhere?" asked Annie. A rough-cut stone arch reached out into the pond from the beach they stood on, and rested its other end on a large lichened boulder perhaps fifteen feet from shore.

"Not to nowhere," said Kiyoshi-chan. "To *there*."

So they stepped up on the bridge and walked out to its end, where so many bright orange carp came to meet them that the water seemed to boil with fish.

"Wow," said 'Siah.

They looked all around and saw the pond area from a new angle, as if it were a new pond. It was ringed with autumn trees of all kinds, and yellow and red leaves drifted down and floated on the surface of the pool.

"Is it still April?" wondered Q.J.

"Who knows? Let's go on," said Annie.

"Just what are we looking for?" asked Owen Greatheart. "Do we have any idea?"

"I don't," said Annie. "Do you?"

Returning to the path they went on, every turn bringing a new revelation, an unexpected landscape under an ever-new season and kind of daylight. Under a bright noonday sun, there was a simple shadowless expanse of rippled white gravel, heaped here and there with mysterious cones of silver sand. There was an early morning hillside of dewy junipers, sculpted into unearthly, fantastic forms and gleaming with the dawn light as if bejeweled. Under a slate December sky there was a miniature black pine in a wooden box, surprisingly dusted with light snow. There were riots here and there of camellias, azaleas, rhododendrons, chrysanthemums. There was a painted, windswept pavilion overlooking a wildly overgrown pool, backlit by a sad westering sun. There was a morning grove of weeping cherry trees, trailing fragile blossomed streamers in the spring breeze.

It was all heartbreaking, exquisite, evanescent, like Life itself.

"This is too much," said Owen Greatheart, almost resentfully. "This is *much* too much."

They came to a low bamboo gate and opened it, finding a small secretive garden space. There was a streambed of multicolored round pebbles, covered by a shallow, unrippled run of clear water. Larger stones, low dark green red-berried bushes, giant ferns, clustered hemlocks, and one squat goose-like stone lantern crowded the little stream, creating spaces of ambiguous reflection and meditative shadow. The shrouded stream drew the children's eyes in, up its jumbled mossy bank to the dark delphic grove from which it fell.

"Just *look* at this," said Annie, flinging herself down on the ground. "The trouble with this is not that it's just beautiful. *Beauty* I can handle."

"I know what you mean," said Owen Greatheart.

"I don't," said Knuckleball. "Explain."

"Well," said Annie, "it's the way that all of this has of looking like it's so significant. As if it's all hiding something that we're supposed to *know*."

"Exactly," said Q.J. "Every new landscape I see here, something in me says Yes! That's what I've been looking for all my life! But then I still can't figure out what it is I was looking for all my life, even though it seems to be right in front of me."

"Little Harriet," said Libby. "*That's* what we're looking for."

"Well, of *course*," said Annie. "But I know just what Q means. It's like a poem that means more than its words say, but you can't figure out the meaning no matter how hard you try."

"It frustrates me," said Owen Greatheart. "I feel like there's something wrong with my eyes, as if I'm seeing things but not really seeing them."

"Just the surface of them," said Q.J. "It almost makes you want to see something that's just plain *pretty* in a simpleminded sort of way."

"Is there really any such thing?" wondered Annie. "I don't know if I'll ever be able to see something as *simply* pretty again. I'll always be wondering what I'm missing."

"I wouldn't have missed seeing the Garden," said Owen Greatheart. "Don't get me wrong. But I do wonder if it might not be spoiling us for real life."

"I don't think so," said Q.J.

"You know," said Annie, "you get the feeling that if you could only hit on the key to this Garden, everything in the Universe would make sense."

"Kind of like all the answers to everything are hidden here," said Q.J.

"No!" said Annie. "Kind of like all the *questions* are hidden here. I don't think I even know the right things to ask yet."

"Seems to me," said Owen Greatheart, "that if we

stayed here for a thousand years, we might finally learn the right questions."

"Then we could start on the answers," said Libby.

"We'd be pretty old by then," said Knuckleball.

No one spoke for a moment, listening to the whisper of the stream.

"Well, *I* have a question," said 'Siah, loudly. "Where is the bathroom?"

"Oh, my," groaned Owen Greatheart.

"Pick a tree," said Q.J. "Any tree."

"Do you think the Garden will mind?" asked Owen Greatheart, taking 'Siah by the hand and leading him out of sight. The other children lay quietly on their backs, watching the tree branches waving far above them, until the two boys returned.

"Well," said Libby, "Now *I* have a question."

"Nearest tree, Squib," said Q.J. "You're a big girl. You're on your own."

"Not *that*," said Libby. "I just want to know how all this is helping us find Little Harriet."

"I don't know," said Annie. "For that, I think we're just at the whim of the Garden. All we can do is wander, and wait, and poke around."

"How about if we chase a chipmunk?" suggested Libby. "Just like Little Harriet did, back in Boston? Maybe chipmunks are some kind of guides to the garden gateways."

"*Great* idea, Squibbles," said Q.J. "We'll wait here. You go chase a chipmunk."

"I intend to," said Libby. "I'm gonna start with that one right over there."

So she lit off after a striped little fellow that was sitting on an old gray boulder, and as if pulled after her by a cord, all the children leaped up laughing and went along with the whimsy, following the tiny beast on a mad and merry chase, round and round, in and out. And who knows whether what followed was the simple caprice of the Garden, something special about that little chipmunk, or something else altogether? The fact is that when they finally clambered after the nimble creature up the stream and up the mossy bank and over the top into a soft pungent tumble of fern and evergreen needles and autumn leaves, they suddenly felt the ground dissolving away under them so that they gasped and caught each other's hands.

"Here we go!" cried 'Siah, and the Garden came rushing out and over them like an irresistible flood, a green and gold and silver tsunami of beauty and undiscovered mystery, sweeping them far, far, far away to another world where none of them had ever been before.

CHAPTER 15

The Arena

They stood at the joining of two long hallways, which ran away from them at right angles to each other. The hallways had floors of fine pale *tatami* mats, and high ceilings of simple polished wood. Each of the two hallways was at least as long as two football fields, and as wide as two mats, perhaps wide enough for four people to walk side by side. In the distance the children could see where the hallways seemed to corner again at sharp angles to run toward each other, as if they formed a huge square. The walls along the outside of this apparent square were of white plaster, interrupted at intervals by great polished, unpainted pillars set into the plaster, as big as trees. Light came from unreachable latticed windows near the ceiling, covered over with *shoji*, undecorated rice paper. The inside walls were entirely different, not walls at all, but sliding *shoji* doors running the whole length of the hallways.

There was no garden in sight, not even a potted plant.

And there were no visible exits.

The first impression of the place was of utter vacancy and stillness. Only gradually did they become aware that there was a deep hushing sound all around them, like the voice of the ocean, or of a vast audience waiting for a performance to begin.

The children realized that they were still holding

hands tightly, scarcely breathing. They exhaled all at once and looked at each other.

"Well," said Libby. "Here we are."

"This is a beautiful place," said Owen Greatheart. "Look at the ceilings. We can see ourselves in them."

"What do we do now?" asked Knuckleball. "Which way do we go? Looks like we have two choices."

"That's one more than we had down in the mine, right, Lib?" said Q.J. "I say let's go to the right."

"That's because you are American, and always go right," said Kiyoshi-chan. "You even drive on the right side of the road, and read from left to right."

"That's true," said Annie. "Somehow it does seem *right* to go *left* this time."

Everyone agreed, and set off down the hallway, with 'Siah and Basho having a somersault race to the first corner. But as it turned out, right or left made no difference, because when they had turned three sharp corners and walked four lengths of hallway, they ended up right back where they had begun. All four sides of the square hallway were identical, without exits or reachable windows.

"Hm," said Owen Greatheart, with a frown. "This is strange."

"Curiouser and curiouser," said Q.J., like Alice in Wonderland.

The ocean-like hum around them seemed to have grown a little louder, and in fact seemed to ebb and flow a bit, with individual sounds in it.

"I think that *is* a crowd," said Knuckleball. "It sounds like Symphony Hall just before the concert begins."

"Except there's no squeaky tuning going on," said Libby.

"I wonder if Knuckleball could reach that window if he stood on my shoulders," said Owen Greatheart. "He could poke a hole in the rice paper and tell us what's outside."

"You can't just go poking holes in somebody else's *shoji!*" said Annie.

"Why not?" said Owen Greatheart. "You want to just sit in here forever?"

"Of course not," said Annie. "But we're certainly not desperate enough yet to have to go poking holes in *shoji*."

"And besides," said 'Siah, "I don't think that noise is coming from outside. I think it's coming from *there*." He pointed toward the inner wall of sliding doors, which up till now they had ignored. The paper doors stared blankly past them, as if asking to be overlooked.

"Well," said Q.J. "I think he's right."

"Easy enough to check," said Owen Greatheart, and he walked over boldly and slid a door open a few inches. It moved with only a whisper in its polished wooden track, but a surge of other sounds leaped through. Owen Greatheart exclaimed something incomprehensible, and jumped back, sliding the door shut with a sharp snick. He looked at everyone, wide-eyed.

"There's a million people in there!" he whispered. "Unbelievable!"

"What do you mean a million?" said Libby. "How could you count them that fast?"

Owen Greatheart ignored her. "There's not much light in there," he said. "But it's a *gigantic* place, full of *people*."

"So let's go in," said Q.J. "They'll hardly notice eight more people, in the dark."

"And one monkey," said Basho.

"And one monkey," said Q.J., scratching him behind the ears.

Owen Greatheart took a deep breath. "OK," he said. "I just wasn't expecting that. But I guess we're here to find things out. Just open the door a crack, and try to sneak in. I think it will be less noticeable if we just do it in one quick rush, rather than opening and closing the door more than once. I'm not kidding, this is a crowd like you've never seen."

They did just that, slipping in the open door and pulling it quickly shut behind them, then slithering side-wise into a secluded nook, behind high-backed seats. They huddled there on what felt like smooth stone or concrete, and waited for their eyes to become accustomed to the dimness around them.

When they finally began to make out shapes, they could look only up, because of the high-backed seats. Only a foot or two over their heads, they could make out the dark forms of thick, carved roof beams and rafters thrusting their way into the stone of the wall. There seemed to be a whole forest of great beams extending out into the deep shadows above them, laid together in a complicated arrangement like trees fallen haphazard together, and spreading out and away from them in a roof of unthinkable dimensions.

"I don't like looking up," whispered Libby to Annie. "It looks like giant spiders could come crawling down out of there."

"Don't be silly," said Annie.

"Well, maybe not *giant* spiders," insisted Libby, "but I'll bet there's at least a billion spiders of all sizes up in those rafters."

"Stop it," said Annie.

"If any of them falls on me," Libby promised, "I will scream at the very top of my lungs."

"*Stop* it," said Annie.

To the left and to the right of them, as far as they could see, there was the back of a row of seats, and nothing else but a stone ledge, running along behind the seats to a distant corner. Over the seats, without standing, they could just see the tops of heads, tipping toward each other and bobbing, as if having conversations. The crowd noise, which out beyond the *shoji* doors had sounded like the sea, now sounded like what it was, a deep mumble of many voices.

Kiyoshi-chan was the first to have the courage to move, crawling carefully over to the nearest gap in the seats, perhaps ten feet to the right. When he got there, he peeped around the seats, gasped, and clapped his hands to his head in astonishment.

"What is it?!" hissed Owen Greatheart. Kiyoshi-chan gestured fiercely to them to come and join him. As quietly as possible, they made their way over to him and looked for themselves. They stared in awe.

Spreading out and down from them in all directions was the vastest indoor auditorium any of them had ever seen. Rows and rows and rows, levels and levels and levels of high-backed, slatted wooden seats filled the huge arena, and every one of them was filled. Here and there, hanging by ropes from the distant rafters, were great paper lanterns embellished with cryptic characters, giving out a subdued light that barely seemed even to reach the murmuring audience. The stone slab on which the children knelt dropped away from them in a long narrow staircase, one of many that streaked the sides of the arena, all coming together far below.

The brightest light came from the center of the whole dark, cavern-like place, where a raised flat platform of some kind was lighted by many lanterns. Above it was suspended a huge wooden covering, an indoor roof resembling a Shinto shrine, that must have weighed many tons. Giant tassels of different colors hung from each corner of the suspended roof.

Even the American children knew enough to see that this whole vast arena served only one purpose.

"That is the *dohyo* and *tsuriyane*," said Kiyoshi-chan, in a whisper of high-pitched excitement. "The wrestling ring and the sacred roof over it. There is no sumo arena on *Earth* like this one. This is an *unbelievable* place. I have been to Grand Sumo Tournaments in Osaka, Nagoya, and Tokyo, but I have *never* seen such a place. Think of it! This whole place, just for *sumo!*" He was almost beside himself with delight.

The other children looked around, impressed, though they could hardly feel the intense excitement of Kiyoshi-chan.

"This must be a *dohyo* for the gods," said Kiyoshi-chan. He clutched his head again. "Maybe this is where the god Takemikazuchi wrestled Takeminakata and won the Japanese islands for our people!"

"Look!" said Owen Greatheart. "Something's happening!"

And indeed, from a faraway arch came a column of what must have been the most gigantic sumo wrestlers who ever existed. Their size was unfathomable because of the great distance across the arena, but even from their perch up near the roof, the children could tell that these were not merely mortal *rikishi*. These were gargantuans from another dimension, mountains of flesh who would have dwarfed Akebono or Taiho on earth. These wrestlers came marching down the aisle toward the *dohyo* with ponderous dignity, their splendid embroidered aprons swaying before them. Every one of them wore the thick white braid of the *yokozuna*, the grand champion. This was to be a tournament of champions like no one on earth had ever seen.

"Ohhhh!" breathed Kiyoshi-chan. "If I died now I would be happy, having seen this."

"No, you wouldn't," said practical Q.J. "Don't be ridiculous. You've been around Knuckleball too much. You're starting to exaggerate."

Knuckleball poked her, but Kiyoshi-chan ignored the comment. "Look!" he whispered again in higher excitement than ever. The huge wrestlers had climbed to the *dohyo* and formed a ring around it. "They're beginning the opening ceremonies!" he said, barely trying to keep his voice down any longer. "I can't believe I'm going to see this!"

But as it happened, he never would. His excited whispers had finally begun to attract attention, and the ancient wooden seats began to creak with impatience. Finally one of the spectators, grumbling deeply, thrust his head around the end of the row to see who was making the annoying hissing noises.

The children cried out in terror. For there, scarcely two feet away, was the black, gaping mask and helmeted head of a demon warrior. Seeing them, he roared with anger and leaped from his seat. All around, more and more goblins jumped to their feet to see what was happening.

"No!" cried Kiyoshi-chan.

"Run!" said Owen Greatheart.

They fled along the stone walkway at the top of the arena, and now could see that the entire vast audience were demon warriors, armored in every possible combination of colors. The disturbance was arousing more and more of the hideous spectators.

"Where can we *go?*" wailed Libby.

There was only one direction to run. Going back into a hallway without exits would be of no use at all. Owen Greatheart swung Libby onto his back. "Hang on, Squibber," he said, and jumping up into the low rafters, he disappeared into the dark shadows of the roof. Basho swung along after him, hand after hand. Kiyoshi-chan followed, then Knuckleball, then Q.J. 'Siah leaped onto Annie's back and she went nimbly after the others, just snatching her long legs out of the reach of the pursuing demon.

Too thickly built to follow the children up into the intricate jungle of rafters, the demon warrior roared his anger after them. The awareness of the human intrusion spread like a flame, and soon the whole multitude of hideous warriors were on their feet shouting, and the noise pounded against the roof like an armored fist. Even the huge *rikishi* in the ring were distracted from their ceremony, and peered out of the brightness of their platform to see what was happening. The children scrambled and swarmed higher and higher into the shadowed rooftop, until they could look down a terrifying distance onto the top of the roofed *dohyo*. Finally, out of breath, they stopped to rest.

"Well," panted Knuckleball. "This is just a great idea, Owen. I always wanted to spend the rest of my life sitting on a rafter like a pigeon."

"I didn't hear any other suggestions," said Owen Greatheart. "Let me know if any occur."

They sat in somber silence, looking down on the insane scene, trying to collect themselves and calm their pounding hearts.

"If a spider falls on me," said Libby, "I'm gonna jump."

CHAPTER 16

The Demon Warrior Makes Promises

"Silence!" thundered a great voice. "Silence, I say!"

The uproar in the enormous arena was so loud that the demand for silence had to be boomed over and over and over before the demonic clamor finally died down. Even then there continued an outraged muttering, like the tumble of rocks in a sack. The children peered down through the rafters to see who was speaking with such authority to a million goblin warriors.

Far below them they could see a single armored figure, standing in the aisle, out from under the *tsuriyane* so he could look up into the shrouded rooftop.

"Keep still," whispered Annie. "I'm sure they can't *see* us up here."

"Human intruders!" cried the demon warrior, standing with sword drawn and feet planted wide apart. "Do you hear me?"

The children shushed each other with unnecessary forefingers on their lips. No one was about to say *anything*.

"You can hardly escape us up there forever," shouted the demon. "*Answer* me."

The children clung to the rafters in absolute stillness.

"You've trespassed upon a sacred place," cried the

demon, waving his arms with exaggerated indignation. "No common creatures can freely witness this great tournament of grand champions. *Who do you think you are?*"

There was an explosion of wings in the faraway reaches of the rafters, hundreds of feet away from the children. A sizeable flock of what looked in the dimness like pigeons blundered their way to new perches in another part of the roof. Thousands of watching goblins whirled toward the sound. Even the huge spokesman, far down on the arena floor, turned toward this new spot, as if the children were there. It was a comfort to have those hideous masks turned away from them, as if a physical grip on the children had been released.

"What could have spooked those birds?" whispered Q.J. "Do you think goblins have gotten up into the rafters?"

"No *way*," hissed Annie. "They're much too big. Look how small these spaces are. It's like a giant latticework, made of tree trunks."

"It takes nothing to spook a bunch of brainless pigeons," said Owen Greatheart.

"Maybe just a rat," shrugged Knuckleball.

Libby squeaked in horror, and clapped her hand over her mouth.

The great demon was still talking toward the rafters on the other side of the arena.

"Listen, human *vermin*," he bellowed. "We cannot allow you to witness this sacred tournament, which is only for the entertainment of gods and demons. But come down quickly and we will let you go without harm. If we have to come up after you, I make no promises."

"Ha!" whispered Owen Greatheart. "We've read too many books to be fooled by a line like *that*. What does he take us for?"

There was silence below them, and the huge crowd of armored warriors stared into the roof shadows far away from the children, as if they could will them to the ground. Knuckleball almost snickered at the sight, as if it were a game of hide-and-seek.

"In fact," roared the goblin spokesman, "if you come down we promise to treat you much better than trespassers deserve."

"He is *such* a bad liar," said Q.J.

"We will *give* you things," bawled the demon.

"Like candy and balloons?" whispered Knuckleball. "Goody goody."

"Things more wonderful than you can ever imagine!"

The children snickered more than their position really warranted, but they could hardly help it.

"This guy needs help with his lines," said Q.J.

"In *fact*," boomed the helmeted monster, "if you come down immediately, I hereby promise to give you the thing you want more than anything in the world."

"Yeah, right," said Owen Greatheart.

The voice of the demon suddenly took on a wheedling, confidential tone. "I *know*," he said, "I know what you want more than anything!"

"We want *Little Harriet* more than anything," whispered 'Siah under his breath, with a small sob. "What can you know about *that*, you big loser?"

"And we can give her to you!" roared the demon warrior, clashing his sword against his armor, still peering into the far shadows of the rafters.

The children tingled from head to toe as if from an electric shock. What had he said? There was no way he could have heard 'Siah's whisper.

"Come down!" rumbled the demon. "Come down and we will restore her to you at last!"

"What is he *talking* about?" Annie hissed fiercely.

"Look at me!" shouted the demon. "Look at me! Don't you know me, little human maggots?"

And the children looked, and for the first time saw that the armor of the great spokesdemon was red and blue.

"He's the one!" said Q.J. "He's the one who stole Little Harriet! He's the one!"

"*Rats!*" hissed Knuckleball. "And all this time I've been hoping it was *his* block I knocked off."

"I wish I had a big rock," said Libby. "To drop on his big ugly head right now."

"The little creature you seek," roared the demon, "is intended as a sacrifice to the gods. Her lot has been drawn, and we took her from the world of men to make a sacred offering. But you can still save her, and *only* you! Your last chance is almost gone!"

The children clung to the rafters in agony, trembling with anger and fear and horror.

"How do we know they're not bluffing?" said Q.J., her voice shaking. "She got away! How do we know they have her again?"

"We don't," said Annie. "We don't."

"Decide now!" roared the demon.

"We don't have a choice," said Q.J., her logic sorting through things quickly. "We can't stay up here forever, they'll get us sooner or later anyway. If we come down now there's a ninety-nine percent chance that they'll do something horrible to us. But if there's only a one percent chance that we can still save Little Harriet, we *have* to do it. All the other choices are closed. This is the *easy* kind of decision. It's only got one choice."

They all thought for just a moment.

"You're right, Q," said Annie. "As usual."

"This is your last chance!" blustered the demon.

Annie leaned over the edge of the great rafter and looked what seemed to be miles down at the huge red-and-blue demon.

"Hey!" she cried. The hideous audience whirled back toward her voice as if it were one person, with a clamorous clash and outcry of voices.

"Hey, you!" she said. The gigantic spokesman of the demon warriors, the kidnapper of Little Harriet, looked upward toward her voice. His mask had the same gaping, ghastly expression as ever, and red flame seemed to flicker around his head. "How do we know you really have her?" cried Annie. "Prove it, and we'll come down."

"Prove it or not, we still have no choice," muttered Q.J. "We still have to come down."

The demon laughed with no humor at all. "Do you doubt the word of a demon samurai?" he bellowed. "Come down now, or the archers will come and *shoot* you down like chickens on a roost. They are on the way now."

"No, they won't," whispered Owen Greatheart. "Or else they wouldn't be trying to coax us down like this. They can't see us up here. *Look* how they lie. Listen, we could lose ourselves in these rafters for months."

"And how many months can *you* go without food,

Owen?" said Q.J. "Think we can live on raw pigeon forever?"

"Or rats?" said Libby. "Or spiders?" She shuddered.

"Why not?" said Owen Greatheart. "Something might happen. Somebody might rescue us."

"Just let Annie decide," said 'Siah. "She's oldest."

"Fair enough," said Owen Greatheart, who really didn't want the honor.

Annie thumped her fist on the rafter in frustration and buried her face in her hands. Finally she leaned over again.

"Here we go," said Knuckleball, rolling his eyes.

"We're coming down!" Annie called in a clear strong voice. "And you'd just *better* have Little Harriet."

"Or *else*," said Libby.

CHAPTER 17

Finding a True Rikishi

The mask of the great demon leered at them as the children were hustled down the long staircase and thrown at his feet. They jumped back upright, indignant.

"So where's Little Harriet?" said Annie. "We came down; you give us Little Harriet. It's the deal."

"Of course," rumbled the towering warrior. "I'm sure you know, though, that it could never be quite as simple as *that*."

"Of course not," said Owen Greatheart.

"We're dealing with *gods* here," said the demon warrior. "They expect their sacrifice, we give it to them. We sometimes play a few games along the way, to keep life interesting."

He crossed his massive arms while his demon audience chuckled with ugly humor.

"What are you talking about?" said Annie. "Just tell us what we have to do to get her back, and we'll do it."

"Well," said the giant warrior, "it's like this. I'll give you a chance to rescue your little creature, but I can't make these substitutions lightly. No matter how generous I am. There are just two tests you have to pass before you get your Little Harriet. That's all." He chuckled again, a terrifying stony clatter inside his armor, and looked around at the watching demons. "Hahaha! I do love to play this game with humans."

There was a crash of horrible laughter at this, and the demon warriors all stamped their armored legs.

"The old impossible quest," said Owen Greatheart. "Like Jason and the Golden Fleece. Well, I'm glad you're having a wonderful time."

There was another roar of amusement at this, but the demon spokesman in red and blue bent down closer to the children.

"Oh, you misjudge me," he rumbled in what was supposed to sound like a sympathetic tone. "Impossible quests?" He straightened up and bellowed with laughter again. "Hahahahaa! How can you think that?" He bent down again. "Oh, no, human trespassers, I promise you that neither of these little tests is *impossible*. At least not in the *usual* sense of the word."

The crowd howled with delight again, as the children held their ears.

"Get on with it," said Q.J. "Stop playing your stupid games."

"Yeah," said Knuckleball. "What's the first test? Let us at it."

"It is simple," said the demon. "The gods would appreciate it if we would first entertain them with an honorable competition. A sumo match, perhaps. The gods *love* sumo, you know. It gets their attention like nothing else."

The children looked at each other, puzzled.

"So where's the test in that?" said Owen Greatheart. "We just sit here and watch a sumo match and then move on to the next test?"

"Hey," said Knuckleball to the demon. "Maybe there's a real softy under that ugly exterior of yours. Did you ever think of that?"

Something inside the demon warrior rumbled like a subterranean blast furnace. Knuckleball ducked behind Owen Greatheart.

"You misunderstand," growled the demon. "One of *you* will have to *participate* in the bout. The rest may watch, of course. If there are any left to watch."

"Now, just a minute," said Q.J. "There were several parts of that that I don't think any of us quite understood. I think you'd better explain."

"Of course," said the demon. "It's like this. There are very few things that can get the attention of the gods for a piddling matter like your Little Harriet. One of those is a true sumo match, involving one of the people in need of divine assistance. One of you, in fact. You win, the gods might just consider rewarding you."

"I'll wrestle *anybody!*" cried 'Siah. "I can knock anybody over!"

The demon guffawed again, even as he searched around his feet to see which of the little ones was speaking.

"And Owen lifts *weights*," said Knuckleball. "We call him Nautilus for short."

"Cool it, Knucklebrain," said Owen Greatheart.

"Hang on again," said Annie. "Just who would our guy wrestle?"

The demon gestured toward the ring of huge yokozuna above them. "Take your pick," he said. "Any one of them would be a worthy opponent." The multitude of demons rumbled again with amusement.

"You are out of your mind," said Owen Greatheart. "That would be like trying to wrestle Mount Fuji. Don't we get someone our own size?"

The demon shrugged. "There is your choice," he said, pointing again. "Choose the smallest of them, if you like."

"Very funny," said Owen Greatheart. "I don't *see* a smallest one."

"What about all of us at once?" said 'Siah. "All together we must weigh as much as one of those guys."

"No way. Maybe a *quarter*," said Annie. "This is so idiotic. It's so *male*."

"Good point," said Q.J. "Where are all the *female* demons?"

"Home," said Annie. "Changing little demon diapers."

"Maybe there *aren't* any female demons," said Knuckleball.

"More than likely," said Q.J. "Almost by definition."

"Maybe all these guys just popped out of somewhere by spontaneous generation," said Knuckleball. "Out of sewer scum or something."

"Look," said Owen Greatheart. "This conversation is all very educational, but I might as well get on with what we have to do." He turned again to the demon. "Where do I go? Up on this platform thingie?"

"Not so quickly," chuckled the demon. "Before you go any farther, you have to understand that this is a very special *dohyo*." He gestured toward the raised earthen ring behind him. "You see, not just *anyone* can wrestle in this ring." He inclined his head respectfully toward the ring of massive *yokozuna*, who bowed in return. "If anyone tries to set foot on this *dohyo* who does not have the spirit of a true sumo wrestler, a true *rikishi*, he will be struck down as soon as he sets foot there. The gods will destroy him."

"Nonsense," said Annie.

"We don't believe you," said Owen Greatheart.

"As you like," said the demon. "Believe it or not, the only one who can participate in this bout is one of you who has the true *rikishi* spirit, and who can therefore safely stand under this *tsuriyane*."

"I think we can safely ignore all this superstitious nonsense," said Q.J. "I agree that Owen is our best bet. He's the biggest of us all, and he *does* lift weights."

"I don't lift *that* much weight," said Owen Greatheart. "But of course I'll do it. What choice do we have?"

"Why are we even going along with this?" said Annie. "Look at the size of those monstrosities. What chance does Owen have against any of them? It's so *futile*."

"On the bright side," said Knuckleball, "it may be *futile*, but at least I never heard of sumo being *fatal*. You have a pretty good chance of surviving, Owen."

"Thanks a lot, little brother," said Owen Greatheart. "But don't forget, this *is* life or death for Little Harriet."

They had almost forgotten this aspect of things for a moment, and grew sober at the memory.

"Maybe I can get lucky," said Owen Greatheart. "Maybe the guy will trip over his own feet and I'll win."

Nobody laughed.

"*Sumimasen*," said Kiyoshi-chan politely, stepping forward from behind Knuckleball. "But you are all making a very foolish choice."

They all turned to him. "Well," said Annie. "It's not like we *have* a choice."

"You're wrong," said Kiyoshi-chan. "We have *seven* choices here. We could choose Annie, or Owen Greatheart, or Quiddity Jane, or Knuckleball, or Libby, or

Josiah. Or," he said, "we could choose Kiyoshi-chan."

"Don't choose *me*," said Basho the monkey, covering his head. "I don't have the spirit of a *rikishi*, no way."

"But Kiyoshi-chan," said 'Siah. "You're one of the littlest ones here. Only Libby and me are littler than you. What chance would *you* have?"

"And what chance does *Owen* have?" insisted Kiyoshi-chan. "None of us have a chance at all. So we can choose freely among all seven hopeless choices. And of all the hopeless choices, I would have the *best* chance." He bowed suddenly, embarrassed at this putting-forward of himself.

"But Owen's the biggest and strongest," said Annie.

"What good will that do?" said Kiyoshi-chan. "How could he even set foot on the *dohyo?* The gods would strike him down without even looking. He doesn't have the spirit of a true *rikishi.*"

"Hey!" said Owen Greatheart.

"He doesn't mean it that way, big brother," said Knuckleball.

"No, no," said Kiyoshi-chan. "I don't mean that you're not strong enough, or good enough, or brave enough. I know you are *all* brave. Q.J. saved Libby from the falling stone, and Libby saved Q.J. from the cave. Owen saved 'Siah from a beating ("A *pretend* beating," said Owen Greatheart) and 'Siah tried to beat up demons coming up out of the ground, single-handedly. Annie tried to tackle a charging *oni*, and Knuckleball knocked his head off with a fence post. But," he said earnestly, "having the spirit of a true sumo wrestler means more than courage. It means certain things about sumo itself that it would take too long for you to understand."

"Well," said Owen Greatheart, "I'm willing to take a chance on that stuff about the gods striking me down. I don't believe any of that."

"But I *do*," said Kiyoshi-chan. "At least I believe that it *could* be true. Sumo *can* be fatal, you see."

"And what about you?" asked Q.J. "Do you think *you* have the spirit of a true *rikishi*?"

"I hope I do," said Kiyoshi-chan shyly. "When I wrestle I feel like I *become* the great Taiho. And Taiho could beat any of these big tubs." He swung his arm at the silent row of *yokozuna*, who were one by one stepping down from the platform and seating themselves with great dignity around it.

"You have no chance," said Annie.

"Neither does anyone else," said Kiyoshi-chan. "But even the littlest *rikishi* has a better chance than no *rikishi*."

The American children shrugged, not liking this at all. Only Knuckleball seemed to understand, and he punched Kiyoshi-chan in the shoulder for encouragement.

"So who will you choose to fight?" said Knuckleball. "Eenie-meenie-minie-mo?"

"No eenie-meenie-minie-mo," said Kiyoshi-chan. He pointed to the big demon *samurai*, who had been listening to this whole conversation with his arms folded across his chest. "I will fight *him*."

There was a clamor of amazement all around at this audacious statement. The huge demon started as if he had been stung in the rump by a bee.

"You can't do that," said the demon.

"Why not?" asked Kiyoshi-chan.

"Because!" said the demon. "You have to choose

from these thirty *rikishi* before you!" He gestured toward the silent sitting ring of wrestlers.

"Who says?" said Kiyoshi-chan. "Did the gods tell you this?"

"That's the way it's *done*," blustered the demon. "You pick him, you fight him."

"And I pick *you*," said Kiyoshi-chan.

"I will not fight a little bucket of spit like you," said the massive warrior. "I would be *degraded* by it."

"I can see only two reasons why you would not fight me," said Kiyoshi-chan. "First, you do not have the spirit of the true *rikishi*, and would be struck down as soon as you stepped onto the *dohyo*."

"Not true!" roared the demon warrior. "I have an even greater spirit, the spirit of a demon *samurai*, and the gods would never strike me down! Just look at this!"

With incredible agility and strength, he leaped backward from his standing position, turning two somersaults in the air and landing on the *dohyo*. He roared and blustered from there, clashing his sword again on his armor. Finally he settled down.

"He is *so* male," said Annie wearily.

"I see that you are not struck down," said little Kiyoshi-chan to the warrior. "Then I only see one other reason for you not to participate. You must be *afraid* to fight me."

The hubbub that followed this was indescribable. The demon warrior stood there thunderstruck, as the vast goblin audience shrieked and rumbled in a mixture of wrath, amazement, and wild laughter.

Knuckleball leaned over toward Q.J. "There's another possibility," he whispered in her ear.

"Maybe he has a weakness of some kind that he's afraid Kiyoshi-chan has figured out."

"Yeah, right," said Q.J. "Wishful thinking."

"I will not do it!" thundered the great warrior from the platform. "Even to *listen* to this is to lose face! Choose one of these great *yokozuna*, you little toad, or don't fight at all."

"I choose you," said Kiyoshi-chan stubbornly. "And I appeal to the *gyoji*."

For the first time the American children noticed a silent figure standing on the far side of the *dohyo*, so still that it seemed almost like a wooden sculpture. It was dressed in a high-necked robe of subdued red, richly embroidered and sashed. It wore a lofty black hat of curious shape, and held in its hand a stiff fan with a purple tassel hanging from it. The figure bowed toward the children, and the stern face smiled.

"Hey!" said Owen Greatheart. "It's the old priest! What's he doing here?"

"Here," said Kiyoshi-chan, "he seems to be a *tate-gyoji*. A sumo referee of the very highest rank. He must be a great priest."

"I *guess*," said Owen Greatheart. "He does keep popping up, that's for sure. Could he be a traitor? He seems to be in thick with these demons. Why else would he be here? I thought he saved Q.J.'s life, but maybe that was all a big act of some kind."

"Who knows?" said Kiyoshi-chan philosophically. "Regardless, I have appealed to him. If he rules against me, I will have to fight one of the *yokozuna*. If he rules for me, the demon warrior will have to fight me. Even the demon will not resist the ruling of a *tate-gyoji*."

"What's the big difference?" asked Owen Greatheart. "Will you have a better chance against that big lug than against one of *them?*"

Kiyoshi-chan shrugged. "Not really," he said. "But it seems more fitting. And I like the fact that he doesn't like it at *all*. That has to help me, somehow."

It was true that the great demon warrior, obviously chafing in indignation, still seemed to hold the old referee in respect, and waited for some indication of a decision.

"Well?" he grumbled finally. "Will you make me go through this farce and demean my dignity as a *samurai?*"

"I will," said the old priest, smiling. "But I'm not sure who is demeaned by it."

The demon rumbled again, deep inside the blast furnace of his chest. "You go too far!" he gritted. "You make me wrestle a puling child."

"But a puling child," said the old priest, "with a great spirit. Prepare for the bout."

The arena was filled with an astonished jumble of conversation as the audience realized what had happened. The children looked around with apprehension. For the demon audience to see their great captain being humiliated in this way seemed to have turned the mood uglier than ever.

"Here we go," said Kiyoshi-chan. Then the little Japanese boy walked over to the earthen platform and tried to climb up onto it. He struggled there kicking for a moment before one of the enormous *yokozuna* leaned over, put a vast hand under his bottom, and flipped him onto the *dohyo*. The American children held their breath, until Kiyoshi-chan scrambled to his feet and bowed deeply in return. The wrestler bowed back, chuckling.

"Well," said Knuckleball. "I guess he must be a true sumo wrestler. He didn't get frizzled when he touched the ring."

"Now, don't you go getting superstitious on us, Knuckler," said Q.J., but even she sounded relieved. "Nobody was going to get struck down by any old gods. That was all just a stupid joke by that big bozo."

"Maybe," said Basho the monkey.

CHAPTER 18

Kiyoshi-chan
Does His Best

It was a ludicrous sight.

On opposite sides of the *dohyo*, the giant armored warrior and the little Japanese boy, like some sort of carnival mirror images of each other, went through all the prefight rituals, the rites of purification and preparation.

Kiyoshi-chan had watched so much sumo with so much concentrated attention, and had imitated every movement so many times with his friends, that he went through all the ceremonial stamping of feet, clapping of hands, rinsing of mouths, and tossing of salt without a slip. Without the Little Harriet factor, the sight of the scrawny little boy acting like so much of a *yokozuna* would have seemed like the most farcical of comedies, and apparently did seem so to the demonic audience, who despite their annoyance couldn't keep down their rumbling laughter. Even the huge impassive wrestlers seated directly around the ring smiled slightly to watch it.

It was something of a surprise to see the gigantic demon taking this part of the proceedings with as much seriousness as his little opponent. A couple of times, however, he paused in midmovement, as if distracted or preoccupied.

"He's still really peeved," said Annie. "He does *not* want to be up there. He's having a hard time keeping his mind on what he's doing."

"The key to the whole thing," said Knuckleball very seriously, "is the *tachi-ai*, the first charge. If Kiyoshi-chan makes a false start, it's all over. I don't know if they'd give him a second chance."

"It's all over anyway," said Q.J. "And how did *you* become such a sumo expert?"

"I had a good teacher," said Knuckleball, adjusting his glasses to squint at her. "A teacher with the spirit of a true *rikishi*. And I still think Kiyoshi-chan knows something we don't know."

"So how long does the fight last?" asked 'Siah. "Does Kiyoshi-chan lose when the other guy holds his shoulders down for three seconds or something?"

"You're getting it confused with American wrestling," said Knuckleball. "As soon as somebody steps out of the ring or part of his body touches the ground, he loses."

"But that could take just a few seconds!" said Libby. "You mean it's all over in a few seconds?"

"Maybe," said Knuckleball. "But I think Kiyoshi-chan has something up his sleeve."

The pre-bout preparations reached the *shikiri* stage, where the two sumo wrestlers usually try to intimidate their opponents while gauging the right moment for battle. Back and forth Kiyoshi-chan and his giant opponent went, from their corners to the lines in the ring, squatting, glaring at each other, returning to their corners. Something about the seriousness of the little boy seemed to be affecting both the giant demon and the audience, making it more difficult for them to laugh at the ridiculous situation. A strange sense of anticipation descended again over the arena.

"How long will this go on?" asked Annie, about the incessant glaring and squatting and returning to corners. It all seemed like an incomprehensible repetition of rituals.

"Who knows?" said Knuckleball. "See how the referee is holding his fan? That means that they can begin whenever they're ready."

"Won't someone give a signal?" asked Libby. "Blow a whistle or something?"

"Nope," said Knuckleball, smugly, forgetting that he had once asked Kiyoshi-chan exactly the same question. "They just have to *sense* the right moment to begin."

"Weird," said Owen Greatheart.

But even as he said it, there was a roar from the crowd as the two opponents came up from their crouch and charged at exactly the same instant. Kiyoshi-chan smashed into the huge armored demon and almost bounced off onto the ground, which would have been the end of it.

"Grab his leg!" shouted Knuckleball. "Grab his leg and just hold on!"

But proud little Kiyoshi-chan had no tricks up his sleeve, despite Knuckleball's hopes. He was just full of being Taiho at the moment, and had completely forgotten that he was Kiyoshi-chan. As Taiho, he tried to jump up high enough to grab the demon's belt for one of the standard sumo holds. The demon slapped him away, playing with him. The crowd laughed.

"Forget that stuff, Kiyoshi-chan!" cried Knuckleball. "Try some *tricky* sumo! Just grab his leg!"

Again and again Kiyoshi-chan tried to fight the demon like Taiho would have fought him, and again and again the demon pushed him away playfully. The goblin arena rocked with hideous mirth. Full of the pride of the *rikishi*, Kiyoshi-chan could think of nothing but losing honorably, and the playful scorn of the demon charged him with anger.

"Forget that, Kiyoshi-chan!" shouted Knuckleball in despair. "Forget being Taiho! Just be Kiyoshi-chan, and grab his stupid leg!"

"What good would that do?" said Owen Greatheart. "It'd just take him longer to lose."

"Yeah," said Knuckleball, "but the longer he takes to lose the more chance there is of something *happening*."

"Like what?" asked Owen Greatheart. "Earthquake? Tidal wave? Asteroid attack?"

"Well, just *maybe!*" yelled Knuckleball, suddenly angry. "Just maybe so! Sometimes you just have to hang on as long as you can, and hope something happens. That's the way life *is*."

The older children could hardly help laughing at this philosophical statement, but then they wondered why.

"I suppose the big guy *might* trip and fall," said Owen Greatheart. "Beat himself, sort of. Can demons have heart attacks?"

"I still think Kiyoshi-chan has a plan," said Knuckleball, with evaporating hope. "But I don't know why he's doing all this suicidal jumping around. What good will that do?"

"You little idiot, Kiyoshi-chan!" Annie yelled, with no hope of being heard. "Stop fighting for yourself! You're fighting for Little Harriet! Just hang on for dear life, and stop trying to be a hero!"

By a trick of coincidence, there was a lull in the crowd noise just as she shouted, and against all odds Kiyoshi-chan heard her words over the roar of the crowd. He felt shame suddenly sweep over him, from head to toe in a scalding rush. Taiho abruptly vanished, and Kiyoshi-chan became just a skinny little boy trying to knock over a twelve-foot demon warrior. Casting away all his *rikishi* pride, he flung both arms and legs around the trunk-like leg of his enormous rival, and held on with all his might.

"*Now* what" he cried. "Does anybody have a plan?"

"Oh, my," said Knuckleball to his brothers and sisters. "I was sure hoping that *he* did."

The audience was laughing more loudly than ever, as the demon warrior stomped comically around the ring with Kiyoshi-chan clinging to his leg. "It's *so* obvious what that big lunkhead's strategy is," said Q.J.

"Does he need one?" said Annie. "Looks like he can just win whenever he wants."

"But he *can't* just win," said Q.J. "That's his *problem*. Kiyoshi-chan's challenge put him into a no-win situation."

"How?" asked Owen Greatheart.

"Just think about it," said Q.J. "He's humiliated if he wins, he's humiliated if he loses. He's been embarrassed as a *samurai*, dishonored, unless he handles this right. And there's only one way to handle it right."

"Which is?"

"Treat the whole thing like a big comedy routine," said Q.J. "Look at him! He's on stage."

She was right. The big demon was hamming it up for the audience, standing on one leg, pretending to lose his balance and just catching it at the last second, spinning around like a top.

"See that?" said Q.J. "He has to convince everyone that he never took Kiyoshi-chan's challenge seriously, and is just being a good sport. That's his only way out."

"But that could backfire on him," said Knuckleball.

"Of course it could," said Q.J. "Look at him! I think he really did almost trip himself that time. All it takes is one slip, and Kiyoshi-chan's the winner."

"That's not what I'm *talking* about," said Knuckleball. "I mean that sumo is serious business, and this is a sacred *dohyo*. He *can't* get away with making it all a big joke. He can't let it go on *too* long."

This seemed to make sense, but the big demon warrior, desperate to save his endangered honor, was going to new lengths to amuse his audience, at one point even leaping into the air for another double somersault, landing on both feet. Kiyoshi-chan held on through it all, his face crushed into the rough lacings of the armor.

Knuckleball was thinking hard. Something about the impossible lightness of the demon warrior's leaps had triggered something, an elusive memory, something that it seemed he should know about these demons. Frustratingly, whatever it was kept slipping around the net of his thoughts, escaping him. He pulled his glasses off, jammed the heels of his hands into his eye sockets, and stooped over, thinking, thinking, thinking.

"Are you OK, Knuckles?" asked Owen Greatheart. "Does your stomach hurt?"

"I'm *thinking*," said Knuckleball through his teeth.

He thought back to the demon's reaction to Kiyoshi-chan's challenge. For a moment, incredibly, it had seemed like real fear. What could such a massive demon have to fear from such a little boy? *He has a weakness*, thought Knuckleball. *What on earth could it be?* The audience was still laughing at the comic scene on the *dohyo*, but the laughter was beginning to seem strained. At any moment the great demon would realize that he was overdoing it, and would have no choice but to fling the little boy out of the ring and be done with it. Knuckleball ground his fists into his eyes, and beat his head with his knuckles.

And then, just when he had almost given it up, the memory he had been waiting for came sliding back, clear as crystal. Just as every baseball player forever remembers his or her sweetest swings, the perfect crack of certain memorable hits, the coming together of bat and ball and arm and body in a rare and unforgettable harmony, Knuckleball suddenly remembered the swing of a certain fence post, the crack of contact, and the head of the demon rolling away down the road.

"That's it!" he shouted, straightening up laughing and flinging out his arms. "That's it!" His brothers and sisters stared at him, aghast.

"Have you finally completely lost it, Knucklehead?" asked Annie. "What in the world are you crowing about? Our representative is about to get *tossed* here."

"He's nothing but an empty suit of armor!" said Knuckleball, jumping up and down. "Remember that helmet, Annie? *There was nothing in it!*"

"You're *crazy*, Knuckles!" said Q.J.

But Knuckleball leaped off the step and pushed his way between two gigantic *yokozuna* to get to the edge of the ring. No one paid him any attention. Looking up, the boy felt more dwarfed than ever by the enormous demon, towering over the *dohyo*.

"Kiyoshi-chan!" he hissed. The great demon was standing momentarily still, trying to gauge the audience, obviously aware that the moment was coming to finish off this absurd bout. Kiyoshi-chan had his eyes squinched shut, but he heard Knuckleball's whisper.

"*What?*" he said, not opening his eyes.

"The old *wedgie-dashi*," Knuckleball said. "Give him the old *wedgie-dashi!*"

"I don't remember *wedgie*," said Kiyoshi-chan, in a pathetic voice. "I don't remember what you're talking about!"

"Never *mind*," said Knuckleball, trying in vain to remember the Japanese word for the proper *kimari-te*. "You just have to lift him *up*. You have to get your feet on the ground and *lift*. Hurry! He's just an empty suit of armor! Don't wait for a scientific explanation! *You can lift him! Hurry!*"

There was no time to think. Kiyoshi-chan suddenly swung his feet to the ground and planted them. Before the great demon had a chance to react, Kiyoshi-chan wrapped his sturdy arms around the massive leg and lifted with all his strength. He staggered, but to the astonishment of everyone, the huge warrior was suddenly hoisted off the ground and wobbling there in midair, windmilling his arms for balance.

"Augggh!" he roared.

Even a suit of *samurai* armor that large is heavy, being made mostly of iron laced together with linen thongs, and Kiyoshi-chan staggered again under the weight. It still felt like real flesh and sinews inside that flexible armor, and the little boy almost collapsed from his own disbelief of what he had done. The towering warrior was trying desperately to reach down and grab at the little boy's grip without losing his balance completely.

"Now flip him!" cried Knuckleball. "*Flip him over!*"

With a mighty grunt and heave, the little Japanese boy pulled the demon's leg out from under him. Like an iron tree toppling, the enormous warrior crashed roaring down on his back.

"We did it!" cried the American children, pounding each other on the back and pumping their fists in the air. "We won! We won!"

Kiyoshi-chan looked back at them, panting and grinning, his face very red. He jumped down from the *dohyo* and rejoined them without a backward look. But after a few minutes of joyful shouting, they all suddenly fell silent, realizing that except for their celebration, there wasn't another sound in the whole ominous arena. They all looked back toward the ring. The red-and-blue suit of armor was creaking its way to a sitting position, and the hideous mask was staring in their direction, with flickers of red flame licking around it. The old priest, in his red referee's robe, had withdrawn to the side of the ring again, and stood as still as before the bout.

Annie looked back into the ugly mask of the demon warrior. "OK," she said. "We passed the first test. What's next?"

CHAPTER 19

Finding Little Harriet

A bell tolled somewhere far away. The arena vibrated with the sound, though it was not loud. There was an irresistible resonance to it, as if the bell was one of those giant temple bells, struck with a swinging suspended beam, that could cause still ponds to ripple miles beyond the reach of their sound. As it faded away, the great red-and-blue demon warrior on the *dohyo* fell backward and lay still.

The children looked around, bewildered. In every seat there was still a demon warrior, but there was no longer any movement or conversation. Thousands of masked helmets stared straight out from the high-backed seats, in row after frozen row. Each demon sat erect, hands on his knees, like a painted stone sculpture. The paper lanterns still glowed with their dim mysterious light, far overhead, pulsing with the fluctuations of their inner flames. All else was still. The four great tassels at the corners of the *tsuriyane*, red, white, black, and green, hung completely without movement. The thirty *yokozuna* sat lotus-fashion on the floor, their eyes half-closed as if in meditation. The red-and-blue warrior lay on his back on the *dohyo* floor, apparently lifeless. Even the red-robed *gyoji* seemed frozen in place, but when Owen Greatheart looked at him, he blinked and moved.

"This was the easy test," quavered the old priest, coming to the edge of the platform and smiling down at them. "The harder one is coming."

"But who's going to make us do it?" said Annie, looking around. "Seems like the creatures who wanted to hurt Little Harriet are all sort of out of action."

"True," said the old priest. "These are evil, malicious beings, more than empty suits of armor but not much. They are no further danger to you for the time being."

"So all we have to do," said Q.J., "is to find Little Harriet and go home."

"Some things cannot be stopped once they are set in motion," said the old priest. "It will not be as simple as *that*."

Owen Greatheart looked at the old priest. "Seems like I remember the chief demon saying something like that not very long ago," he said. "Who are you anyway? Are you in some kind of *alliance* with scum like this?"

"Very much like it," said the old priest. His meaning was not at all clear. "It can't be helped."

"You don't ever answer a question directly," said Owen Greatheart. "Why not?"

"Why do you have such a hunger for direct answers?" asked the old priest. "A direct answer is never what it appears. But ask me a question, and just for you, this once, I will give you a Direct Answer."

"Where is Little Harriet?" blurted Q.J., before anyone else had a chance to speak. But she knew that was the question on the tip of every tongue, and when she saw the priest smile she knew that he also knew it. She wished for a fleeting second that she had asked something different, unexpected, just to shake that exasperating expression, that serene look that was so much like omniscience. But she knew also that no other question mattered.

The old priest turned away from the *dohyo*, toward a long ramp that led under a section of seats toward a massive wooden door. It was down just such a ramp that the thirty *rikishi* had earlier marched, from the other side of the arena. He glanced back at them. "She is on the other side of that door," he said.

Without waiting to see if he was following, they raced up the ramp, hearts pounding.

"It'll be locked, wait and see," said Owen Greatheart, still the skeptic. "Why else would he have told us?"

But when they got there, they found that the door, big as it was, had a simple sincere latch, and no lock. They heaved it open and ran through, but fell back, blinded, finding themselves in bright sunshine. Before them was a wide wooden walkway, with painted railings along either side. It was covered by a carved ceiling, but its sides were wide open to a warm ocean of wind that poured across it from right to left. It extended ahead for perhaps a hundred meters, where it touched the top of a mountain. The mountain itself was like a bread loaf set on end, a heap of gargantuan stones and ancient evergreens that seemed to defy every known demand of gravity. Its sides tumbled away downward for thousands of feet, into a misty valley where the white bed of a rocky river was occasionally visible. Hawks soared below the walkway.

"Whoa!" said Knuckleball. "I can't do this. Even *stepladders* make me dizzy." He staggered back to hold onto the door frame.

They looked back through the door and down the ramp toward the old priest. He was dimly visible in the shadowed arena, silhouetted against the comparative brightness of the *dohyo*. They could see the prone form of the huge demon captain on the *dohyo* itself, and faint impressions of the uncountable rows of demon statues in the seats. The old priest gestured to them in a way that seemed to mean to go on. They looked back again into the sunlit world ahead of them.

"OK," said Annie. "This seems to be another one of those easy choices. Straight ahead."

'Siah and Libby scampered on ahead, shouting with delight, running to the railings to look down into the depths. Basho the monkey followed them, climbing pillars, swinging along on the outside of the railing, leaping through the ceiling rafters of the walkway, seeming both to be sharing in the little children's foolery and making sure they did themselves no harm. Annie and Q.J. each took one of Knuckleball's arms and hustled him along, with Kiyoshi-chan alongside.

"Oh, my," Knuckleball said, trying to cover his eyes. "I think I'm gonna be sick."

Owen Greatheart brought up the rear, having closed the door with one last careful look back at the mysterious old priest. He sauntered along with his hands in his pockets, thinking deeply, his baggy jeans snapping in the breeze. The wind was as substantial as food and drink, full of the whole world around them, as warm and enveloping as a tropical sea.

When they finally reached the far end of the walkway, Knuckleball ran to the nearest tree and hugged it. "I do love solid ground," he said.

"Look!" said 'Siah, pointing back. "Look where we just came from!"

When they looked, they saw no sign of the huge arena that should have stood there. At the end of the walkway was a massive door, set into the side of another mountain like the one they were on, but that was all.

"On," said Annie, pointing toward the only path, a narrow stony one that twisted away ahead of them over the piney crown of the mountain. "Little Harriet must be ahead somewhere."

At the crown, they had to pause again.

"Wow," said Owen Greatheart. "Unbelievable. The ocean."

Invisible from the other side of the mountain, they could now see the deep green sea sweeping out in all directions to the horizon. Far below them, they could see where the ocean and land came together, on a beach that looked from where they were like a litter of boulders.

"On," said Annie again, not to be denied.

The path went over the crown, but then began to descend steeply. The children ran downhill where they could, but in other places had to clamber down the steep faces of stones that filled the path. Down and down they went, racing through the pine grove shadows that crossed their path like cool currents in a warm lake, tumbling down steep places, pausing only for moments to catch their breath. Two or three times they surprised deer in the pathway, who leaped away at their coming. As the time passed they began to feel the muscles on the front of their thighs begin to cramp up, and to tremble uncontrollably when they stopped. By this time Owen Greatheart had a weary Libby on his shoulders, and Annie and Q.J. were taking turns with the exhausted 'Siah.

"We can't stop," said Annie. "Something horrible is in motion, and we can't stop until Little Harriet is *safe*."

They plunged on down the mountainside, becoming more and more reckless in their haste. They began to find signs of human habitation, tiny shrines by the way or little uninhabited human shelters. The path was obviously carefully maintained, and even the larger evergreen trees along the lower slopes of the trail were pruned of their dead lower branches.

"Another time," said Owen Greatheart, "we'll have to do this climb more slowly, so we can appreciate it."

"Right," said Annie. "Another time."

The trail finally leveled out enough to have occasional flat stretches, which were better than rests for their weary legs. Still the tendency of the trail was always downhill, and though they could not see out away from the mountain, they could tell from occasional glimpses that they were still a good distance from the valley floor.

It was when they rounded a bend in the trail, a sharp turn marked by a tall thick pine that blocked the view beyond it, that they saw their first human in this wind-washed land. Almost out of sight ahead of them, on the same trail, they glimpsed a patch of dark clothing and the unmistakable swing of a human stride. At this sight, they ran ahead shouting, but the person was invisible after the next bend. On they plunged, still shouting, until they could clearly see the dark form ahead, strangely far away but perhaps closer than at first. Down and down the trail they went, not really sure why it seemed so urgent to catch up to the person, but unwilling to give up the chase. Finally they bowled around another large pine tree and stopped so abruptly that they ended up in a heap. There was a dark-robed figure standing there in the pathway ahead of them.

"Oh," said Owen Greatheart, the disappointment deep in his voice. "It's *you* again."

It was indeed the old priest, dressed again in his former priest's robes. He also wore an extraordinary straw rain hat that came halfway down his back.

"Yes," he said. "You need me, so here I am."

He would say no more, but lifted Libby from Q.J.'s back onto his bent old shoulder, and set off again down the trail.

"A path without bypaths," he finally said, breaking a long silence that had fallen over the whole group. "Isn't it lovely to have only one choice? Enjoy it while you can."

It was after many more windings of the way that the old priest finally led the seven children to the bottom of the valley floor, across an arched stone bridge, and onto the stony rubble of the beach that they had first seen from thousands of feet overhead.

"Ah!" said the old priest, setting Libby down on the ground and rubbing his hands together with satisfaction. "Here we are, at last." He peered out into the ocean, as it came brawling its way again and again through the rocks onto the beach. He shaded his eyes and squinted far out to sea. "And there, at last," he said, "is your Little Harriet."

CHAPTER 20

Impossible Choices

"Where!" cried Annie, thumping on the thin shoulder of the old priest. "Where is Little Harriet? Are you out of your *mind?*"

"Perhaps," said the old priest. "But there is Little Harriet."

No one could see anything in the raucous tumult of surf. Here and there they could see vertical stones standing out of the ocean, but there was no sign of any human life. Sea gulls dipped and sobbed on the sea breeze.

"She is beyond the sight of any of you," said the old priest. "But she is there, on the ancient stone of sacrifice. At the highest tide it is six feet under water. Many children died there in ancient times, sacrificed to the gods. It has been long since a child died there."

"How do you *know* this?" shouted Owen Greatheart.

"I was told it by the demon chief himself," said the old priest. "I am not omniscient. I know only what I am told."

"Why are you just telling us *now?!*" cried Annie. "Why didn't you tell us *sooner?*"

"This was the soonest you could have come here," said the old priest. "Knowing *this* would only have made you more reckless on the way, and may have thrown you into some other danger. It is not always best to know things."

Q.J. flung herself at the old priest. "Then why are you telling us now, at all?" she sobbed. "There's nothing we can do now. After all this, our Little Harriet will die *anyway?*"

"There is a boat," said the old priest, infuriatingly serene. "One boat, around that bend. It is an old boat, but there are no holes in it. It is in a calmer cove, away from this riot of waves, where you can pull out away from shore."

Before he had even finished, all seven children were running in that direction, stumbling over stones, falling, skinning their knees, getting up again, and running on. The old priest moved after them without apparent haste, and because he never stumbled he got to the boat at the same time the first of them reached it. It was an ancient flat-bottomed fishing boat, full of old nets, with two curiously shaped oars. The old priest and smaller children tumbled into the boat, while the older three pushed and shoved it off the shore, falling into it at the last moment.

"Tell us where to go," said Owen Greatheart roughly, taking one of the oars. Annie took the other, and they began to pull together.

"Three degrees north of that standing stone," said the old priest, pointing. "Many yards past it you will come to the stone of sacrifice."

"How much time do we have?" asked Q.J. "How much time till the rock is covered?"

The old priest considered, looking at the lowering sun and the shoreline. "Perhaps thirty minutes," said the old priest. "Perhaps a little more. It is more than enough time, even against the waves."

The two oldest children bowed their backs into their work.

"We'll get there faster than that," said 'Siah. "Owen lifts weights."

"But then we'll go in circles," said Knuckleball, who knew something about rowing. "Because Annie *doesn't*."

"Ha!" said Annie, taking this personally. She hauled away on her oar with such fury that the boat began to curve in Owen Greatheart's direction, and he had to catch up. There was no conversation for a long space, as the boat began to make progress out toward the stone of sacrifice and Little Harriet.

"I have to tell you one more thing told me by the demon chief," said the old priest at last. "There is one more truly horrible thing set in motion by the demon warriors."

"What could be more horrible than what they've already *done?*" asked Owen Greatheart through his teeth. "You talk, we'll row."

"If you look to the north," said the old priest, as if a great weight were on him, "you will see a railroad cutting in the mountainside, beyond this bay, and a bridge spanning the end of the bay itself."

"I see it," said 'Siah, squinting in that direction.

"Me, too," said Libby, competitively, perhaps a second before she really had.

"Me, too," said Knuckleball and Kiyoshi-chan, almost in unison.

Q.J. just looked hard in that direction. "So what?" she asked.

"When the demons set your Little Harriet on the rock," said the priest, "they set a trap for you that could only have been conceived in Hell."

Annie and Owen Greatheart kept pulling on their oars, but something in the voice of the old priest cast a dreadful suspense over the boat.

"What do you mean?" asked Q.J., in a cold voice. "And make it *quick*."

"When they placed her on the rock," said the old priest, "at the same time the demon chief had other demons unbolt one of the rails of that bridge. When a train passes over that bridge at high speed, it will surely be derailed."

There was total silence in the boat. Annie and Owen Greatheart kept rowing.

"It will plunge into the ravine," said the old priest. "Everyone on the train will die."

Annie and Owen Greatheart still pulled at their oars, but more slowly.

"So *what?*" said Q.J. "Tell us *everything*."

The words seemed to have to be pulled by force from the mouth of the old priest. "There is a train," he said, "an express, due to cross that bridge. Soon."

"How soon?" asked Q.J.

"In about thirty minutes," said the old priest.

"So," said Q.J. slowly, "we would have time to go and signal that train before it crosses the bridge?"

"Yes," said the old priest. "A little more than enough."

"Or," said Q.J., "we would have time to reach Little Harriet and rescue *her*."

"Yes," said the old priest.

"But not both," said Q.J.

"Not both," said the old priest.

A deeper darkness than ever seemed to rise up in every heart, a hopelessness before impossible choices.

"Will *all* the people on the train die?" asked Libby.

"Surely so," said the old priest. "The bridge is high, and there are great rocks below it."

"How many people will be on that train?" asked Knuckleball.

"Many hundreds," said the old priest. "Many hundreds."

Q.J. broke into sobs, as if she had been holding out against them for days. She buried her face in her arms and rocked back and forth, back and forth, her body shaking.

"Why did you have to *tell* us?" Owen Greatheart lashed out at the old priest. "Why couldn't *you* have made the choice, and just not told us the alternative?"

"It was not my choice to make," said the old priest. "Because Little Harriet is not my Little Harriet, nor are any of the people on the train mine."

"I don't know whether to love you or hate you," said Annie. "Who are you, anyway?"

The old priest made no answer.

All rowing had stopped, and precious minutes were passing.

"Do we *have* a choice?" said Annie. "It's a choice between hundreds of lives, or just . . . ." She couldn't finish.

Everyone was crying, from oldest to youngest.

"But it's *Little Harriet* out there on the stone!" wailed Libby. "She's not just *anybody!*"

Owen Greatheart took the sobbing little girl onto his

lap and buried his face in her hair. "But nobody's just anybody," he said unsteadily. "Every one of those people is a Little Harriet to *someone*."

There was no answer to this, no possible answer.

Annie lifted her face from her hands and tried to speak clearly. "Everyone will die if we don't decide *quickly*," she said. "*Including* Little Harriet. How would we ever live with that?"

"Should we vote?" asked Owen Greatheart.

"Quickly," said Annie. "Time is running out. Youngest to oldest, not counting Kiyoshi-chan. None of these people are *his*, either. 'Siah?"

Kiyoshi-chan fell back against the side of the boat in a wave of relief at this, feeling the burden of decision roll away from him. 'Siah held his head, shaking it, crying and unable to speak.

"What about you, Squib?" asked Annie.

"I choose Little Harriet," said the little girl stoutly, simply. "I *love* her."

Knuckleball was crying, too, but there was anger in his tears, anger against the choices of life, falling on him so young. "Little Harriet," he said. "Little Harriet. We have to save Little Harriet. That's what we're *here* for."

"Q?"

Q.J. sat very still, unable to control the sobs that rocked her body. She raised her tear-soaked face and looked from Owen Greatheart to Annie. They looked back at her for a long moment, then all three nodded. The two oars began to pull again, out into the darkening sea. Stroke by stroke the four strong arms pulled the boat through the water, as swells swept the boat upward toward the sky and then dropped it again. They passed the standing stone pointed to by the old priest, and pulled for what seemed like an eternity away from the setting sun.

Finally the old priest said, "We are very close. Go carefully."

The two oldest children pulled more slowly, while everyone else strained their eyes to see the stone of sacrifice standing up out of the sea. For several awful moments they thought that they were too late, and that the stone was already underwater. But Q.J. was the one to shout the news.

"I see her!" she cried. "There she is! Little Harriet!"

They rowed according to her directions, until they were close to the stone of sacrifice, and could see their little sister standing and reaching out to them, and could even hear her small voice calling across the water. The light of the setting sun fell directly on her, so that her face seemed to shine against the darkness of the dusky ocean. They were in great danger for a few minutes, as they tried to maneuver in closely enough to reach her without smashing the boat on the stone. She reached out to them, almost wild with terror.

"From the lee side!" cried the old priest. "Get around behind the stone, where it leans out over the water. We will have to sweep past quickly, or else we will all die on the rock."

It was impossible to stand in the tossing boat, so Q.J. got up on her knees, as close to the side of the boat as she could get.

"Now *go!*" she shouted, and the two rowers pulled with all their might toward the rock. Swooping down the side of one wave, with more luck than skill they came up right beside the out-thrust part of the stone where Little Harriet stood. Q.J. reached over impossibly far and got a grip on the little girl's arm, just as another lifting wave started to sweep the boat away again.

"Oh, no!" she cried in agony. "I don't have her!"

And Little Harriet, seeing the boat being swept off, pulled her arm away in fear of being dragged down into the terrifying ocean.

"Q.J.!" she cried.

"Quick, Little Harriet!" shouted Q.J., leaning as far as she could over the side of the boat. "Jump!"

Then Little Harriet did the bravest thing of *her* whole life. Casting away her fear, she ran to the edge of the stone and jumped as far as she could toward Q.J.'s arms, while Owen Greatheart and Annie fought with their oars to keep the boat in toward the stone. The little girl screamed as she fell short, but when her tiny dark head bobbed back to the surface, Q.J. seized the little body and tumbled backward with her into the boat.

They wasted no time rowing back toward shore, away from the deadly rock. When safely away, they flung down their oars and hugged and kissed Little Harriet, laughing and crying and laughing and crying again that they had found her at last. But almost immediately Owen Greatheart snatched up his oar once more.

"Come on, Annie," he said. "Let's go."

Annie looked at him one blank moment, then nodded and took up the other oar. They began to row to the north, across the bay.

"We would never forgive ourselves," said Annie, "if this turned out to be the only time the express was late, and we weren't there."

"Whatever happens," said the old priest, "you have chosen between impossible choices. Therefore, you have chosen well."

No one knew how to respond to this, so the two rowers rowed and the others watched the shore creep closer. It was grim work. Q.J. huddled Little Harriet close to her body to warm her, but everyone was silent as the old boat crawled toward shore, with the red sun setting just off the port bow. Stroke by stroke Annie and Owen Greatheart hauled away in perfect unison, as if they had always rowed side by side, in just this way. The shore seemed to get no nearer no matter how they rowed, but they just kept rowing, with their heads down, watching the green water slide by out of the corners of their eyes.

They were still a hundred yards from shore when they saw the sleek silver train, its many windows bright with light, swoop around the bend of the dark mountain and dip downward toward the bridge. Knowing then that it was hopeless, the children stood up in the boat and waved and shouted at the top of their lungs, until they almost swamped themselves several times. Even the old priest shouted like a madman, while Basho the monkey leaped and gibbered in the bow.

"Too late!" cried Annie. "It's too late!"

And before their grief-stricken faces, the doomed train, full of hundreds of folk who were each a Little Harriet to someone, roared down the slope and onto the great bridge.

"No," whimpered Libby. Knuckleball covered his eyes, cringing in horror, not wanting to watch but looking through his fingers.

The crowded train thundered across the bridge and on through the trees, climbing a steep grade before it disappeared safely around the far mountainside.

The boat rocked on the waves, unheeded, as its ten occupants stared after the vanished train, stunned.

"What . . . ?" said Q.J., finally. "How . . . ?"

"He lied to me," said the old priest, his voice cracking with an unidentifiable emotion. "The demon *samurai* lied to me."

"But why?" asked Annie. "Why?"

"Even the gods love to play such games with us," said the old priest. He seemed very tired. "So why not the demons?"

In a great confusion of anger and weariness and overwhelming relief, the children slumped to the bottom of the boat, flinging their arms around each other in an exhaustion of emotion. The old priest stepped carefully around them and seated himself on the central seat, taking an oar in each hand. He looked at them, having recovered his maddening tranquility.

"You hate me perhaps," he said. "But now *I* will row."

CHAPTER 21

Under the Deep Green Sea

The old priest rowed for hours, deep into the night ocean, while Basho the monkey sat in the bow and gazed unmoving at the horizon. The children slept soundly in the bottom of the boat, covered as well as possible by the robe of the priest, who rowed in nothing but his rain hat, a thick wrapping around his waist, and a loincloth. When the sun finally rose, the children sat up rubbing their eyes and looking about in bewilderment. There was no land in sight in any direction.

"Don't worry," said the old priest. "Trust me."

"In our country," said Owen Greatheart, "we are told never to trust anyone who says that."

The old priest chuckled. "That is very good advice," he said, but kept rowing. He rowed through that day and another night and another day, while the children asked no questions but spent all their time sleeping or watching the ocean pass by. There was little to see, but there was something healing about the smooth, steady passage of so much deep green water, and the children let themselves be eased, one bit at a time. The scrawny old man rowed through another night, his arms seemingly tireless.

"We haven't eaten in three days," said Annie.

"Are you hungry?" asked the old priest.

"No," admitted Annie.

"You won't be hungry," said the old priest, "until we get there."

"Where?" asked Q.J.

"There," said the old priest, and no more.

So they finally came There, but where There was the children couldn't tell, nor how this There differed from all the other places they had been on the wide ocean. It also was deep green water, but Basho the monkey leaned over the side of the boat and called, and a vast sea turtle suddenly surfaced beside the boat.

The old priest bowed deeply and spoke to the huge turtle, with great respect. "Please," he said, "take these children to the kingdom of your master, and ask him to care for them as they deserve. I regret that they have seen so much trouble and so little hospitality in our land. They are tired and sore with choices."

"I understand," said the great turtle. "For your sake I am sure that my master will give them great honor."

The old priest bowed. Then the American children stepped from the boat onto the back of the turtle, which was the size of a small island. They turned back to bow to the old priest, to Basho the monkey, and to Kiyoshi-chan, who knew that they were going not only to a far-away place, but also to a faraway time, to the time of strange heroes such as Akebono the unknown *yoko-zuna*, and *No-ma-ru* the unknown shortstop. He wept at the strangeness of it, and at the loss of Knuckleball, who had become the best friend he had ever known.

"Good-bye, Kiyoshi-chan," said Knuckleball. He wanted to say, "I'll see you later," as he would have said upon leaving any other friend, but knew that this time he couldn't say it. Tears flowed down his cheeks.

So they waved and bowed as the turtle sank into the depths of the ocean, and as they descended on its back. As always happens when anyone invited descends to the realm of the Dragon King, they were able to do so without drowning or even getting wet. Thus it was that the great turtle delivered them safely to the gates of the King's palace, and delivered his message to the King himself. Then the American children were taken into the beautiful palace, given into the care of courtiers and ladies-in-waiting, allowed to bathe luxuriously in deep steaming tubs, and given exquisite embroidered kimonos to wear. When they were ready, they were entertained at a great banquet in the presence of the King and Queen themselves, and served an incredible array of *sashimi*, paper-thin slices of every kind of fish all arranged in wondrous and brilliant floral designs, reminders of the flowers of the Garden of a Thousand Worlds. As they ate, musicians entertained them with *koto*, *shakuhachi*, and *shamisen*, delicate instruments of suggestion and significance, their music patterned after the rhythms of wind, rain, sea, and forest. Afterward they watched dramatic performances and spoke with the King and Queen for many hours until the littlest children were sagging with sleep and even the older ones wanted nothing more than a soft warm *futon*. Their first night in the palace of the Dragon King was spent in rooms of white *tatami*, with the sound of the sea beyond the pearl-colored *shoji* doors.

Having been properly tended at last, Q.J.'s ugly injury healed with amazing speed, leaving her without even a scar to take home and show her friends. With this last worry removed, there was nothing to hinder the children's enjoyment of the Dragon Kingdom, and for many days they lived in that palace in great happiness. But sooner or later, as every Japanese tale about that realm records, its visitors always grow homesick. Some say there is something in the magic of the realm itself that causes the homesickness, perhaps to keep the kingdom from being too populated by its guests. But more likely, there is simply something in the magic of home, which sooner or later always draws one back, even from the most enchanting places.

By whatever magic it happens, it happened once again with these children, and they went to the King and Queen and requested a ride home.

"Maybe one of your turtles could drop us off some-where on the West Coast?" asked Annie. "We could call our parents from there, and arrange a way home."

"And in our own time?" Owen Greatheart added. "Could that be arranged?"

The Dragon King and Queen smiled graciously, as they always do in such situations, and taking the four smaller children by the hand, they led them all to an inner courtyard of the palace. There the children found themselves in a little garden that they had visited before, but had no reason to prefer to the many other beautiful philosophical gardens of the Dragon Kingdom.

"*Sayonara*," the Dragon King and Queen said together, releasing the hands of the littlest children and gesturing them all toward a thick stand of green bamboo in the corner of the courtyard. Annie was reminded of the bamboo grove in Kyoto, and was stricken again with regret for how little she had seen, given the opportunity.

But now they were all bowing and saying *sayonara* with growing eagerness, as they backed toward the bamboo grove. As they got nearer to it, they could feel and smell a breeze blowing from it, a hot, familiar Boston breeze that brought tears to their eyes. Then they felt the garden rushing up and outward to receive them, and the last they saw of the Dragon Realm was the King and Queen bowing in farewell, and other friends of the palace peeping around the royal couple to wave and bow.

"I can't wait to get home," said Little Harriet, as they were swept away.

Epilogue

On the second floor of Boston's Museum of Fine Arts, Brenda the security officer decided to change her usual coffee-break routine and take a crisp walk, hoping that this would excite her circulation and keep her awake for the rest of the shift. After a quick circuit through the Egyptian and Chinese galleries, she meandered back toward her post in the Impressionist room. With a moment to spare, she first paused in the exhibition shop and put her round elbows down on her favorite leaning place, the broad windowsill that overlooked the Japanese garden. The sun shone on her face and she relaxed, resting her chin on her right hand. Whatever her walk had done for her circulation seemed to be subsiding, and she yawned an enormous yawn. Thinking that the garden seemed unusually full of children, she yawned again. *Children?* She looked, rubbed her eyes, and looked again, her cheeks quivering.

"*Hey!*" she yelped. "*Hey!*"

She glared into the garden, her nose pressed to the glass.

"*Shoot*," she finally said in a fierce voice, kneading her temples with trembling fingers but not taking her eyes off the scene below her. "I've been working too hard. I've got to get a vacation, anyhow I can."

"*Sumimasen*," said a gentle voice beside her. "Excuse me, please."

She jumped sideways, and looked back to her left in alarm. A short, slight Japanese man was standing at her elbow, with his hands clasped behind his back. He was probably middle-aged, with thinning hair on top and light crinkles at the corners of his eyes. He was looking out of the window as she had been, with an odd smile on his face.

"Please excuse me," he said again, still smiling, "but why do you say that?"

"Say what?" she asked. "I didn't say anything."

"You said," he went on, still looking away to give her a chance to collect herself, "that you have been working too hard and need a vacation." His English was really quite good.

"So?" she said, leaning back on the windowsill as if to reclaim a piece of lost ground. "Everybody says that. Everybody needs vacations."

He shrugged an American-style shrug. "I see," he said. He went on looking at the remarkable scene below them. There was a silence. Then he turned back to Brenda.

"You do see those children?" he asked, smiling again. "The ones in those most beautiful kimonos down in the garden?"

"Sure," said Brenda, with a nonchalant air. "Pretty, aren't they?"

"Yes," said the man. "I would not have thought that there were such kimonos anywhere on Earth."

"Oh," said Brenda, not being expert in such matters.

"Curiously enough," said the man, "Just a few moments ago I saw those same children run behind that stone lantern, dressed in the most ordinary American jeans and sneakers. Then they emerged seconds later in kimonos embroidered by goddesses. Did you see *that*?"

"Hmph," said Brenda, but there was a part of her that was relieved, in spite of herself. After all, how seldom do two perfect strangers lose their minds at the same moment for no obvious reason, only a few feet apart.

The two stood there for several minutes, watching the seven decorative children walk around a bit, as if bewildered, then suddenly start laughing and run for the garden gate. One boy hung back a little. He was about ten years old, wearing crooked glasses, a weatherworn Red Sox cap, and a sea-green dragon kimono that would have been worth a fortune to this very museum. He looked toward the stone lantern with sadness on his face, then turned and ran to catch up to his brothers and sisters.

The Japanese man said something, staring after the little boy.

"Huh?" said Brenda.

The man turned to her. "His name is Knuckleball," he said, speaking the word carefully, with only a hint of several extra syllables. "I knew him once, long ago. He was my best friend."

This puzzled Brenda. "You crazy?" she asked. Her comfort in their shared sanity wavered.

"But there is a sad thing I remember," the man said. "Once I told him that he did not have the spirit of a true *rikishi*."

"Really?" said Brenda. "Whoa. Hard to believe. What's a *rickishy*?"

"He does have it, you know," the man said. He still gazed away in the direction the children had gone. "They *all* do."

"Oh, well," said Brenda, still puzzled but feeling a

small fondness toward this Japanese tourist who had shared her hallucinations. "I've got no explanation for any of this. And I don't admit to *anything* that I've got no explanation for." She chuckled.

The man looked up at her. She was startled to see that his eyes were brimmed with tears.

"Why, sir," she said, "I didn't know . . . I mean . . ."

He blinked quickly, but some tears spilled down his cheeks.

"Funny," she said, "but I always heard that Japanese folk don't cry. Funny the things people think. Course I always knew better. There's *nobody* don't cry."

Still talking, she smoothly handed him a clean tissue from a little plastic package she carried in her pocket. He dabbed at his cheeks with it, as if he had never used one before.

"Thank you," he said. "Thank you very much." He returned to the window. The children were out of sight. With his hands clasped once more behind his back, the strange tourist gazed down into the garden, looking as if he would never move again.

"Well," said Brenda. "Guess it's time to go."

He looked at her and smiled. "Yes," he said. "It's time to go." Then he turned with a quick, decisive movement and walked away.

Brenda the museum guard raised one eyebrow at the empty garden and shook her head, smiling in a small way. "Nope," she said. "I don't admit to *anything* I can't explain." She stretched, yawning again a huge yawn, and went back to work.